FATHER OF MONSTERS

A Norse Loki Fantasy Novella

A.B. Frost

For Angrboda, the mother of the misunderstood.
For Joe who remains my friend no matter how weird I become.
And for my mother Nancy Ellen, my angel in the heavens.

CONTENTS

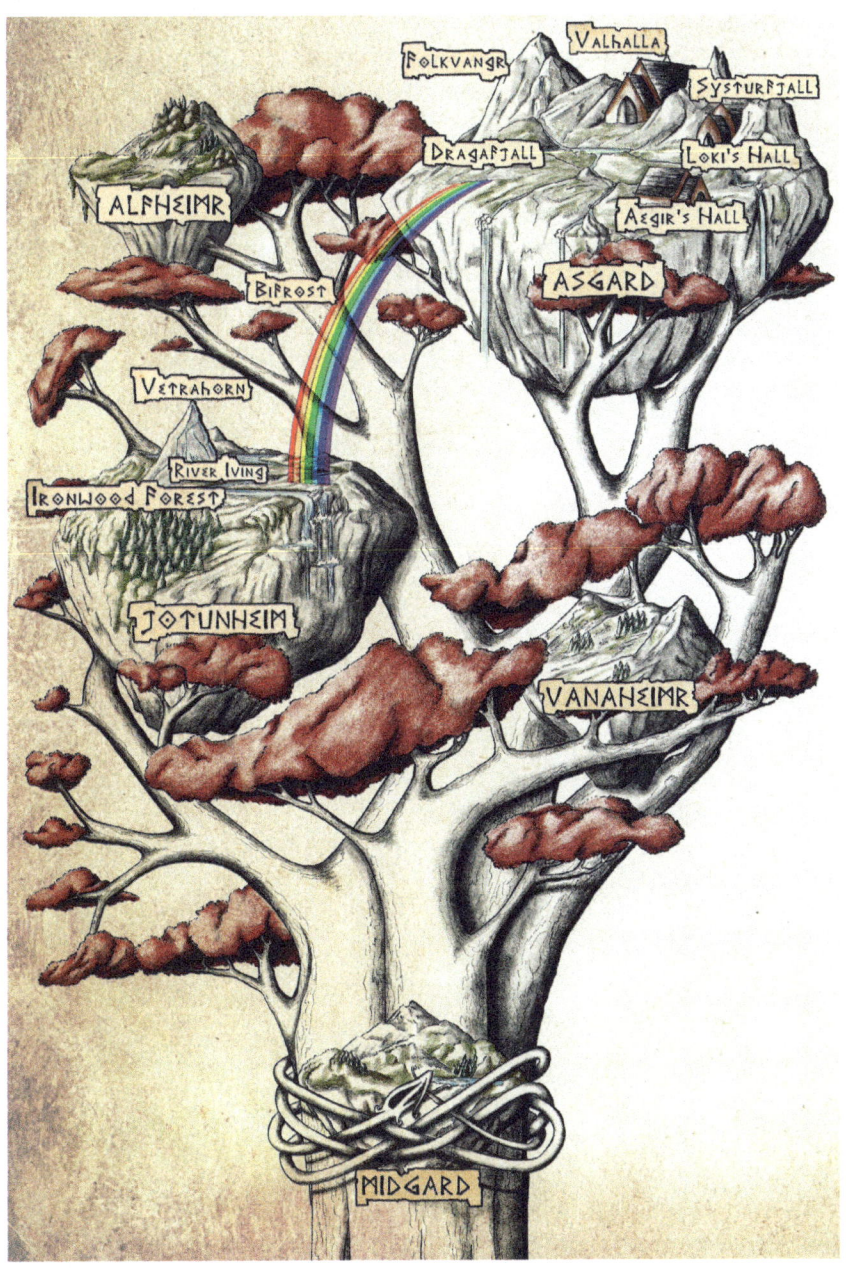

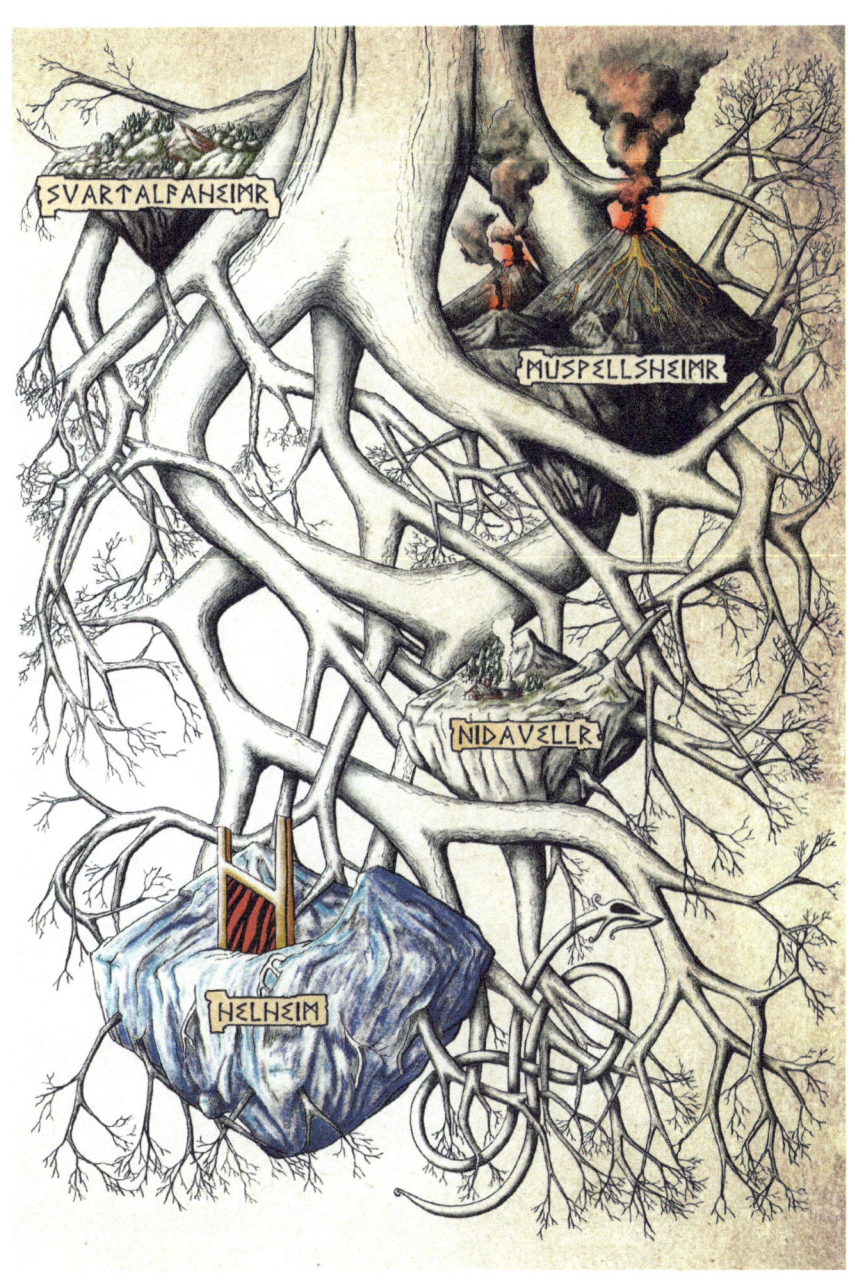

"*The giantess old in Ironwood sat in the east, and bore the brood of Fenrir; Among these one in monster's guise was soon to steal the sun from the sky.*"
—VOLUSPA V. 40

"My purpose is clear."

—LOKI

PART I

ILLUSION AND TRUTH

Illusion is the first of all pleasures and I, Loki, am no stranger to any of them.
Asgard, Home of the Gods—965 A.D., Midgardian Years

It was twilight hour in Asgard and I, Loki, the master of illusion, had little time to spare if I were to adhere to Odin's wishes. Disgruntled that I had agreed to such a trivial task, I tossed the sheets from my naked body, forgetting for a moment about the lovers tangled with me. An empty bottle rolled from under the feathered pillow as I shifted my weight, but I caught it before it crashed to the floor and awakened them.

Quietly, I slung my aching limbs from the bed as a lovely, vanilla-scented silk ribbon slipped off my thighs. The last thing I wanted was to have to explain myself for sneaking away. Odin's demands always managed to curtail my fun, especially when they required my attention first thing in the morning. Last night's unexpected pleasantries had been fueled by my recent growing frustrations about my situation in Asgard—and drunkenness. As enjoyable as the twins had been, it did little to ease my sour mood as I would have to concoct a lie about my whereabouts to the mother of my child.

As I stood, my head began to pound. Picking through the garments scattered about on the floor beside my bed, I began to dress. Dizzied from an abundance of wine, I slipped my arms through my tunic, its fabric cool against my warm skin.

Staring out the window, I watched the sky change colors with dawn's arrival. Time was of the essence. Plotting a theft allowed little room for error, especially when it involved stealing something from a high-born goddess.

Sitting down gently on the edge of the mattress, I reached for my boots. The hand of one of my lovers, a servant named Arne, firmly grabbed my thigh.

"Where are you going?" he asked. Arne was no stranger to my flighty ways. He was a regular late night willing companion.

I glanced briefly at him. No use in lying. "Where else? To carry out one of Odin's bullshit ideas." I brought my hands to my temples in a poor attempt to relieve my worsening headache.

He made a face as if he didn't believe me, an expression I recognized. It was no secret in Asgard I couldn't be trusted. "This early?"

I sighed, impatient about my guests and even more so over the lunacy of agreeing to Odin's request. To be fair, I had been drunk and distracted by my persuasive lovers when Odin talked me into it. The wise old god knew my weaknesses, which he regularly exploited.

"Yes. This early."

"What did you agree to now? Don't tell me it's another journey to Midgard to seduce a king?"

"Unfortunately, no," I mumbled as I laced up my boots. "That would be far more appealing. At least I could get off."

His hand found the curve of my back. My flesh tingled under his touch. "I can help you with that." He sat up. With his hand, he brushed my knotted hair away from my neck, where he placed a gentle kiss. Aroused, I allowed a soft moan to escape me as his lips traveled to my collarbone.

His invitation tempted me. My lust begged to stay and submit, leaving Odin to carry out his schemes on his own. I could sink back into my bed and into Arne. Not to mention remedy this nasty headache and perhaps even sneak off to see my family once nightfall came.

But I couldn't. My yearning to please Odin was even stronger than my yearning for physical gratification. Odin held the key to the one treasure I wanted to unlock—godhood.

With interest, I watched the woman beside Arne stir beneath the silken sheets as she eyed us hungrily.

"Perhaps tonight," I said. That was a lie. Tonight, I had to get back to Jotunheim and the giantess Angrboda, the mother of my son, before she used my head as wall décor.

I stood and made my way across my chambers without looking back. Stepping outside my door, I glanced up at the pastel-purple sky. The air was still. Nothing stirred. There was no one in sight. Perfect timing. Needing the gift of flight for my mission, I shapeshifted into falcon form—an art I had only recently mastered—and one I'd kept hidden from the gods. Only Odin knew, and he already took full advantage of my newly developed magical talents, I didn't want any of the others to join him.

Odin was the ruthless, wise, and treacherous leader of the Æsir and my sworn blood brother. Had I been careless to let him know of my newfound abilities? I'd grown weary of the game we played, in my quest for godhood. His failure to fulfill his promise. Yet, I was still willing to oblige.

Snapping my beak once, I spread my wings and took to the sky above Asgard in pursuit of the Necklace of the Brisings.

It was no ordinary necklace. It was made with magic and crafted by the dwarves, the greatest smiths of all the nine realms. Both dwarves and gods said it was the most beautiful treasure ever made, suited for only a goddess. When worn, it lit the room and protected the wearer. It had been gifted by the dwarves to Freya, the goddess of desire, love, and war.

I had a different opinion of what she was a goddess of —something I'd mentioned one evening in the feast hall when I was drunk. Apparently, Freya took offense at my suggestions, as soon after, our budding friendship soured. Despite the joy I got out of provoking Freya, her threats that evening were enough to scare me into keeping my thoughts to myself, for now.

With a gust of wind, I soared past Odin's Hall, a place known as Valhalla. Valhalla stood at the base of the majestic Systurfjall mountain. Beside it ran seven waterfalls. The river Hvergelmir flowed around it and then branched off into more rivers, eventually leaving Asgard where it fed other realms only to convene as one again in the land of the underworld. Even at this hour, at its entrance stood several of the Einherjar, mortal warriors who had died valiantly in battle and were chosen to spend their afterlife with Odin. I, for one, never saw the appeal.

The wind whistled through my feathers as I banked left, towards the meadow Folkvangr where Freya's Hall stood. In the center of the Folkvangr meadow ran the river Gunnthorin, next to which Freya had built her lavish hall. The golden thatched roof of Sessrumnir glinted in the early morning light, held up by rune-inscribed pillars that sparkled like the stars in the night sky. I personally found the place a bit tacky, but who was I to judge? Freya had her tastes, I had mine, and we rarely saw eye to eye about anything, let alone our opinions on decorating. Luckily, she stayed out of my way, and I avoided her like ox dung in a meadow on a hot summer's day, unless of course it benefitted me.

Perched in an apple tree in falcon form, I knew this was a bad idea. Although I had become more skilled in the art of shapeshifting and illusion magic, sneaking into the home of the most powerful goddess in Asgard to steal her most beloved possession was a risk most would not dare take. Which was why Odin asked me to do it. He knew I was god hungry and wouldn't refuse.

I left the safety of the tree and circled her hall until I found the windows of her bedchamber. I peeked in to see the shape of the goddess tucked under a layer of silk sheets. Another shape was beside her. It shifted enough to reveal her handsome brother, the god Freyr.

This was about to get good. What a scandal. Certain to shake the branches of the proverbial world tree if it found its way among the whisperers of Asgard. I tucked the sight away in memory for later use as incentive for a bribe or two. For now, the necklace. My attention shifted to the only way in, a crack in the window's oak frame just large enough for a fly to squeeze its way through.

Transforming myself from falcon to insect, I slipped in through the crack. The honey-scented air was warm and close and stunk of burning mugwort, an herb that, in larger doses, created hallucinations.

I landed at the edge of the bed beside Freya's face. Her eyelids fluttered as if she were dreaming. With a snort, a blast from her nostrils of ale-stained air blew my fragile insect shape sideways. Regaining my composure, I stepped aside to avoid her golden hair that flowed across her pillows from enveloping me. Beside her, Freyr stirred, shifting the coverlets, revealing bare, glistening breasts. The necklace shone against her skin like buttered gold.

Eagerly, I rubbed my insect feet together and looked about to find two of her colossal sized cats beginning to circle the room. Shit, I had to get this done fast. I took a step toward the prized jewels, readying my jaws to undo its clasp. A growl interrupted my plan. I looked up at a grey paw closing in on me.

I hadn't planned on this.

The paw swiped at me and I launched myself into the air. The feline stared at me, its pupils mere slits. Panicked, I fluttered my wings. The cat swiped again, this time catching my shape, sending me into a tailspin onto the mattress. The last thing I saw was the giant pink, padded bottom of the paw.

"What are you doing?" Freya's voice echoed in the dark as the mattress shifted under me. "What do you have?"

I was caught. My chest wall began to pound. The cat mewed loudly.

Freya's muffled voice came through. "I can never catch

any sleep." A struggle between the goddess and the feline ensued as I grew certain I was about to be crushed to pieces.

"Let it go. Let it go *now*." The cat hissed its defiance as it set me free.

The pressure was suffocating. I gasped. My head swam and I felt myself blacking out. I couldn't think of a less noble way to die. Panic-stricken, I had little choice but to transform myself into something else to escape.

I shifted, realizing almost immediately the form was the wrong choice. As my insect wings turned to feathers and my feet to talons, the cat took a playful swing at my bird form. Freya screamed. The scene transformed into a fury of tumbling feathers, flashes of fur, and tossed bed sheets, with the irritated and red face of Freya at the center of it all.

"What in the nine realms is this? Shapeshifting magic? Who are you?"

Desperate to escape, I took flight but was catapulted backwards like a boomerang as the hand of the goddess grabbed my tail feathers. I shifted my shape again, this time to my own.

Screw it.

I landed, belly down onto the mattress beside Freyr, who woke, appearing stunned.

Freyr stared at me, naked and as red-faced as his sister.

"Hello, Freyr." I winked at the blue-eyed god who looked about as embarrassed as one could.

With a cat writhing in her arms, Freya screamed, "By Odin's spear what are you doing here?"

Rolling onto my back, I casually reached for the drink on her bedside table. "Before you get angry with me—"

The rattling walls proved it was already too late for words to save me.

"You . . ." The cat leapt from her arms as she bundled her

fists at her sides, taut-lipped and shaking. "You are going to answer to Odin for this. I don't care if I have to drag you there by your privates."

"First," I said, "you above anyone else should know I like the sound of that; my privates are quite sturdy and I like it rough. Second, you might want to put on a bit of clothing first. Just a suggestion."

The goddess didn't look amused. Her eyes turned black, and I wondered if that would be the last thing I ever saw.

Freya stomped her bare feet on the floor. The walls shook. A vase tumbled to the ground. Her cats hid beneath the bed. Freyr looked so frightened I thought he might join them.

"That is it, trickster." Her voice was a whisper at first. "I have had enough of you. Come to think about it, I had enough of you when you first arrived in Asgard, which, might I add, was the worst thing to ever happen here."

"I believe the worst thing to ever happen here was your taste in decorating." I fingered the tassels of a gaudy lamp.

"Get your filthy hands off of my things. Who knows where they have been." She pushed me aside.

"No worse than yours." I eyed Freyr. "Although I must say, he is quite irresistible. Even I can't resist the treasures of Asgard." I lowered my gaze to Freyr's chiseled body. The modest Freyr blushed and looked away as Freya shoved me back into a chair.

She pointed a ringed finger in my face. "If you dare to speak one word of this to anyone I will sew your mouth shut again myself. Do you understand?"

"Your secret is safe with me." I shuddered at the thought.

"I will demand that Heimdall take you to Odin immediately to answer for this."

At the mention of Heimdall taking me anywhere my

headache returned. Heimdall could offer to take me to an eating contest followed by an orgy with twins and I would still refuse. Things would get even worse if I had to be escorted by a pompous showboat I couldn't stand the sight of.

"That won't be necessary," I said as I stood. "I can take myself. I'm not crippled."

"You will be once I get through with you. You will be slithering on the ground like the snake that you are!" She tapped her foot on the ground. "And since when have you mastered shapeshifting? Last time I saw you try, you ended up a sightless serpent without a tongue."

"I've been practicing."

"I see."

While clutching a silk robe against her naked shape, the goddess snapped her fingers. At her command, one of her felines left the room through the open window. Freyr stood and began to collect his garments.

"Grooming day?" I asked, my eyes fixed on Freyr's exquisite backside.

"No. I have sent for Heimdall," she said as slipped her arms through the robe.

"Fine, so be it," I replied, assured that once Odin admitted this was his idea I would be off the hook with the furious goddess.

"You sound mighty confident for someone who was caught sneaking around my chambers." Freya crossed her arms and inclined her head. "One can only surmise why you are in here. Was it Odin?" She fingered the necklace and stared at me with narrowed eyes. She knew as well as I that Odin had wanted the coveted gold since it first appeared on her neckline.

Despite my mercurial ways, I would be bound to a rock before betraying Odin's trust. I would leave it up to the wise old god to admit the truth.

"That is not for me to say," I replied as the ground trembled. The watchman was approaching.

Seconds later Heimdall appeared in the doorway, dressed in armor best suited to leading an army through the end of days. "What in the nine realms is—" He paused and looked about the room.

Freya tied her robe, while Freyr hurriedly slipped on his gold and blue tunic. I stood in between them both, delighted that I wasn't the only one to witness the scandal between the siblings.

Heimdall cleared his throat. "Do I even want to know?"

Freya straightened, her haughty demeanor returned. "This pervert was snooping around my hall in the shape of an insect."

Heimdall looked at me and then at the partially dressed Freyr.

I waved. "I'm the pervert?" I gestured toward Freyr. "And he's with me, right, Freyr?"

"Never mind any of that," Heimdall said. "I don't want to know. Loki, it looks like you're coming with me to explain yourself, yet again." He stomped across the floor and reached for me.

Backpedaling to avoid Heimdall's grasp, I knocked into Freya's tasseled lamp, which teetered and crashed to the ground where it shattered. "Oops."

The goddess's face turned from red to a deep purple. "Get out!"

Heimdall reached for me again as I scurried past her. "You don't have to manhandle me. I can follow along."

"I don't trust you, trickster, no one does." Heimdall took me by the cloak collar and shoved me toward the exit of Freya's Hall.

"You're wasting your time, goldie." I was confident Odin would take my side. "Shouldn't you be standing watch at Asgard's gates? Keeping an eye out for invading Jotuns or whatever it is that you do?"

"The only Jotun I have to watch for is you. Which reminds me, lie-smith, I've been meaning to ask where you have been sneaking off to in the middle of the night."

Alarmed about his knowledge that I had been leaving Asgard most nights, I tried my best to sound innocent—a skill I had perfected through the years. "Sneak?" I scoffed. "I beg your pardon, but I don't sneak anywhere."

"You don't?" Heimdall said. "Then why do you leave by way of a secret passage and not by the Bifrost like the rest of us?"

"Secret passage?" I laughed. "There is no such thing. Everyone knows there is only one way in and out of Asgard and that is by way of the Bifrost—you know, that gigantic glowing rainbow bridge between the worlds? The one you stand guard at day and night?"

The watchman huffed loudly. "I don't need you to remind me what the Bifrost or my duties are."

"Well, it seems I do, since you are convinced I have a secret passage. That is not even possible. Odin would see it; everyone would. Secret passage, that is lunacy. Where would you even get such an absurd idea." I was anxious to hear his explanation.

"It's not lunacy if it was hidden with illusion," said Heimdall, "which we all know you are a master of."

"I'm sorry, but did you just call me a master?"

"Of deceit, yes."

"No, I believe you said master of illusion," I replied glibly. "Why Heimdall, I'm glowing."

The god didn't share my sentiment. "It's not something

A. B. FROST

to be proud of. I knew it would only be a matter of time before you used your tricks to deceive us. But you can't deceive me—I see everything, Loki, even the illusions you create. You're not the only one talented with magic."

My heartbeat thumped in my chest. "There are no illusions here, only delusions. Secret passage." I chuckled. "I'm not that good. I am flattered though, truly."

Heimdall wasn't convinced. "And where were you last night?"

"I will have you know I was in my hall last night, tucked in safe and sound with two very willing servants that—"

"That is enough detail. I would rather not hear about what goes on in your hall once the sun sets and the ale flows."

"Suit yourself." Odin's Hall, Valhalla, came into view. "You are too boring for my tastes, and we are too much fun for yours."

"Fun isn't the word I would choose." Heimdall led me by the arm.

"Cunning? Good looking? Funny? Best dressed? Shall I continue?"

Heimdall grunted at my attempt at humor and said nothing more as we made a turn into a meadow.

We walked along the clear, bubbling stream Geirvimul that leads to Valhalla. In the distance, the rainbow bridge Bifrost, which connected Asgard to the other worlds, burned a fiery red, which could mean only one thing. The mightiest of all the gods, Thor, travelled on it.

"Lucky for you, trickster, Thor is leaving Asgard." Heimdall motioned with his chin toward Bifrost. "Otherwise your punishment would be even more painful."

"Doubtful." I was confident Thor would do no such thing. Thor was my friend, quite possibly my only friend in

Asgard, and he needed me too much to ever do me harm. And although I wouldn't dare admit this, the sentiment was mutual. I couldn't say the same for many of Asgard's inhabitants.

Heimdall muttered something, which he knew irritated me.

"What did you say?"

"I said," his voice rose, "I wouldn't be so confident, trickster. Even Thor has grown tired of you."

Although his remark burned, I resisted the urge to ask him to explain. I trusted Heimdall about as much as a fox in a henhouse.

We entered through Valhalla's golden gates. Beside them, a hart moved gracefully around a tree, eating its leaves. Every time it pulled a leaf from a branch, another would grow in its place. In Asgard, everything was eternal.

In a small field, several of the Einherjar met for their morning practice battle. None of them looked surprised to see me in this predicament. In the center of it all lay Odin's home, the biggest of all the halls. Its roof was made of battle shields trimmed with the heads of finely sculpted stone wolves. The god Baldur, Odin's son, stood at the bottom of the stairs as if he expected us.

"Fine day for a walk, isn't it, Loki," he said with a grin. He lifted a large silver cup to his mouth. Steam rose from the contents as it met the cool morning air.

"Why, Baldur," I said, "you look as if you haven't slept in days. I would suggest finding Idun so she could remedy that with one of her apples."

The god of light made a face in reply. Baldur was like the rose in the garden of Asgard— the most popular and the most beautiful, yet a thorn in my side.

Amused, I watched as he lifted the cup to his face to see

his reflection and began smoothing his hair.

"What is your problem with Baldur? He's always cheerful," Heimdall asked as we ascended the stairs.

"That's my problem with him. No one is truly that cheerful all the time."

With a shove from Heimdall, I entered Odin's Hall. The room was lit with torches and light streaming in from tall windows, each framed with golden runes that glinted in the light. A fire burned in the center hearth, and near it, a wooden table had been set with enough food for a feast. Underneath the table lapping up scraps were Odin's two wolves, Freki and Geri.

Upon seeing me, they dropped their scraps and bellowed. Both wolves looked at me with dripping wet jowls and bared their sharp teeth. In the center of the room, seated on the large oak chair named Hlidskjalf, sat Odin. Beside him was a table where he tossed bits of cake for his two ravens Hugin and Munin, who perched atop the high seat.

The birds croaked upon my arrival and I, never fond of the two spies, sent them a crude gesture with my hand, certain they were amused by my predicament.

"You can let go of me now," I said to Heimdall, whose grip had already eased.

He sent me a look before reluctantly releasing his hand from my arm.

Odin's face wore a look of surprise.

"Not what you expected?" I asked Odin as his two wolves approached me as if it were playtime and I was the toy. Fond of them both, I scratched their ears as they howled in delight. I had always wanted a wolf of my own.

"I say we sew his mouth shut again," said Heimdall as he set himself up beside the feast table and lifted a piece of raisin cake to his mouth.

I made my way over to the table as well, purposefully picking at the plate the watchman was preparing for himself. "Looks like I'm not the one who needs my mouth closed," I said as I pointed to Heimdall's tightened belt. With one hand I shoved a piece of the cake into my mouth. "Must be all that standing in one place. May I suggest swimming? I know you love to practice taking seal form."

A spot of cake flew from my mouth and landed on Heimdall's golden collar. The god's face hardened, and he put his food back down on the table. Lifting a cloth to wipe his collar, he turned to Odin. "I'm going outside before I slit this Jotun's throat."

Turning toward Odin, I greeted him with my mouth full of food. "Someone is a bit touchy today."

The old, one-eyed god didn't share in my amusement. Instead, he placed his drinking horn down and folded his hands in his lap with a sigh before sending me a look I hated.

"What?" The wolves eagerly lapped up the crumbs that fell from my hands.

"What did you do, Loki?" He handed his two ravens a piece of raisin cake. He was cunning, a liar, a cheat, and relentlessly stubborn. Despite our relationship being only by oath, we were very much alike, which made for good fun when the mead flowed.

"Nothing you didn't ask me to do," I said casually.

The door slammed. Freya's voice echoed across the hall from behind me. "I caught him snooping around my chambers in insect form." I looked back to see the goddess standing in the doorframe, dressed, her hair banded in rings of gold, the necklace glinting against her tanned flesh. Heimdall stood beside her.

"My, you clean up nicely," I said.

Freya disregarded me, her bejeweled shoes clicking on the stone floor as she passed me. "I wish I could say the same for you." She stood beside Odin and folded her perfectly manicured hands together. "I do believe the punishment for entering the hall of a goddess without permission is death, is it not?" Freya lifted a spear that leaned against the table.

I looked at Odin, who said not a word in my defense, his one cool blue eye avoiding my stare as if I could turn him into stone.

"Not if the interloper was instructed to do so by the lord of the Æsir, right, Mighty Odin?"

Odin appeared unmoved. "That is a bold accusation."

Several other gods arrived in the doorway of the hall as I waited for his explanation.

When it didn't come, I tried another tack. "I beg your pardon, but that isn't an accusation, it's the truth. Tell them, brother, tell them what you asked me to do: steal the Necklace of the Brisings, all because you are jealous that she was gifted it by a dwarf in exchange for—"

With a loud snort, Freya interrupted. "There is absolutely no need to discuss under what circumstances I was gifted this, and let me remind you, Loki, you are not a god but a Jotun visitor, here to serve us. You have no ground to accuse Odin of such things."

Unfazed by her comments, I continued my point. "—sex, with a bit of this as well." I made a lewd gesture with my mouth. "And I don't need reminding of why I am here in Asgard. I am reminded every day with every thankless good deed that I have performed for each and every one of you. Like a dog begging for its master's scraps. Correction—even your wolves get better treatment than I do."

"A dog has better tricks than you," quipped Heimdall.

The flesh of my face burned red hot with anger. How dare Heimdall? And how dare Odin for not admitting the truth. "I thought you were waiting outside? Something about slitting my throat?"

"I thought I should oversee this discussion."

"That won't be necessary, although I know you must justify your purpose here since your duty to stand watch all day is useless now that I had a wall built to keep Asgard safe."

"Surprised you make mention of that, Loki, considering the shameful deed you performed to have it built." With a smile, Heimdall strategically placed his hand on a tapestry woven with an animal's image. The woven fibers depicted an eight-legged horse named Sleipnir, Odin's steed, who also happened to be my son.

The room fell silent. Everyone knew not to mention that event in my presence as it wasn't my finest moment, although luckily it ended well. The gods got their wall and Odin now owned the best horse. Surprisingly, Freya was the first to speak, and it wasn't what I expected.

"Not shameful, but dutiful. Now let us drop the subject and focus on the matters at hand, shall we?"

I looked at Freya, confused as to why she defended me. The goddess glanced at me before returning her attention to Odin. "Odin?"

The one-eyed god continued to avoid my eyes while tending to his wolves, who were still begging for scraps at his side. After what felt like an eternity, he spoke. "Perhaps it's best that Loki and I discuss matters alone."

The gods and goddesses looked at one another before exiting the hall, leaving me, Odin, and his creatures in awkward silence.

Infuriated, I spoke first. "I can see where your loyalty lies, brother, with yourself. How dare you not defend my actions when it was your bidding. Does your treachery have no limits?"

Odin looked indifferent. "Loki, you got caught. That was not my agreement with you."

"No, it wasn't, and neither was this illusion you created that I would someday be a god. I wish I could say I am the master of illusion, but the reality is, I am a mere victim of an illusion you crafted to lure me here."

"You are overreacting. Freya's temper is like a boiling kettle. She will forget all about this once her steam blows off."

"I won't." My hands clenched at my side. "I am made to look like a fool in front of all the gods, and for what? To carry out one of your stratagems that I wasn't even sober enough to agree to."

"You didn't complain last night over drink, or were you too busy getting a hand job from a servant to care?"

I looked down at my hands which burned hot. Traces of fire emanated from the center of my palms. With a deep breath, I bound them as fists at my side.

Odin's eye traveled to my burning fists. "I'm not at fault for what you agreed to, Loki; that was your choice. You came to Asgard on your own free will. You can leave whenever you please," said Odin coolly. "Which reminds me, Heimdall mentioned he found a passageway hidden by illusion near Dragafjall. Know anything about that?"

I froze. "No, I don't."

Odin sipped his wine before replying. "I see. Strange how you seem to be spending more time away from Asgard, yet Heimdall rarely sees you on the Bifrost."

"I travel fast. Heimdall doesn't see everything."

Odin leaned forward in his seat. "But I do. I see every-thing from this seat, Loki, and I know you are going to Jotunheim."

My head began to pound. I did my best to look unfazed by Odin's revelation. "Since when must I ask permission be-fore traveling to other realms?"

"It's not where you are going, Loki, that concerns me. It's why you feel it's necessary to hide it that I fear."

"Perhaps I am seeking some solace in a place where I am understood."

Odin stood. His dark blue robes trailed behind him as he made his way towards me. Sensing the rising tensions, Geri and Freki both circled the nearby table and whined.

As he neared, a chill ran down my spine. He stopped only inches away and placed his ice-cold hand on my face. He whispered his next words. "I hope my own brother would not betray me. That witch can't be trusted, Loki."

I looked into Odin's cool blue eye and in it I saw us. I saw the first night I ever met him, on the Midgardian Sea. In the distance a volcano spewed red hot magma so bright the sky looked as if it were on fire. I saw him carving runes into my flesh with his spear. I saw us together in his ecstasy bound by oath. And then I saw nothing but the glacial blue of his eye.

"Funny you should mention betrayal." Pushing his hand away, I paced the front of the room, the sound of my boots muffled by the fur rug which covered the floor. "You know there is a saying, be careful what you wish for because you just might get it. Well, now I truly understand the meaning of that. You knew how god hungry I was when you lured me here, and you knew how badly I wanted a purpose, and even more, how badly I needed a friend. I'm beginning to think you never meant your promises." Taking a drink from a horn set on the table, I slammed it down before striding from the room.

Odin's voice followed. "Where are you going?"

With my hand on the oak door's golden latch, I paused. My mind traveled to my family, kept secret in a place far away, too harsh and too dangerous for the gods to ever venture.

I never looked back. "To find some solace."

PART II

A MOST UNUSUAL FAMILY

Scars remind us that our past is real.
Asgard—Moments later

F ollowing my heated exchange with Odin I made my way back to my hall. I felt betrayed, fed up, and annoyed that I had even agreed to such a fool's errand. But most of all, I was concerned that the reason for my nightly ventures from Asgard's walls would become public knowledge. You see, Angrboda and Odin had a shaky past. He would never approve of my relations with her, or our unusual child. Nevertheless, I needed to get home to my family.

After a long sleep, I awakened to the darkness and quiet of Asgard's night. For quite some time now, every day, just before the sun rose, I would journey to Jotunheim by a secret passageway hidden by magic. To travel to the middle worlds, the gods used a burning rainbow bridge called Bifrost which Heimdall guarded faithfully. Being as resourceful as I was, I had forged my own way through the willow forests that bordered Asgard's walls.

After peeling myself away from my bed, I dressed and stepped outside. The air was cool and crisp, the dawn sky clear. I stood outside my hall to admire the glittering stars. After a moment of enjoying the quiet I struck out for a short walk to the nearby waterfall Skogafoss which fed a stream behind my hall. Climbing along an outcropping of boulders next to the falls, I reached the tallest rock and waited for the moment when I would make my way to the land of giants, the place my family called *home.*

A cold mist reached my face as I took a moment to inhale the sweet scent of mountain avens that grew nearby. From my perch, my eyes caught the brilliance of two stars to the north that aligned perfectly. A glowing arc of blue swirled around them, signaling to me that it was time to leave. This magical moment occurred just before dawn in all the nine realms. The star known as Sirius converged with another star and amplified all magic. In other words, at this moment anything was possible.

I shifted my shape, feeling my skin grow taut and hot over my body as my own abilities took effect. I looked down at my clawed feet, covered in silver scales, and shook my feathered body loose, preparing to take to the sky in falcon form. Pushing off from the cold surface of the rock, I lifted myself into the air as the gentle spray of water from the falls splashed my feathered face. The sensation of flight was a freeing and glorious thing, which I relished each time as if it would be my last.

Silently, I soared west through the low-lying clouds of mist through Asgard's dawn, watching the ground below for signs of anyone spotting my shadow. But there was no one. Not even Odin's devious pair of ravens. I flew towards the mountain ridge known as Dragafjall where stood a large basalt rock column. Beside it was the gateway to the universe, Bifrost. Behind the column, hidden by day with illusion magic, was a tunnel of crooked willow trees. At that moment I cast my spell. Behind the rock columns the tunnel within the willows appeared. This would be my passage out of Asgard.

With one strong thrust of my wings, I dove toward the forest. Before entering the tunnel of willows, I caught a glimpse of the tan rump of a mare on the outskirts of the wood.

Astride the mare was Baldur, son of Odin, golden boy of Asgard, and the least likely fan of yours truly. I tilted my falcon face toward him as he looked up with his sky-blue eyes. *Bastard.* Was he spying on me? I wondered if this was Odin's doing.

Turning my attention back to the forest, I barely avoided a collision with the trunk of a large oak and was swiftly enveloped in complete darkness as I entered the willow tunnel. Using my other senses to guide me, I dropped low to the ground and felt the warmth of the earth on my tail feathers and let the scent of moss fill my nostrils. I snapped my beak to taste the air until I detected the faintest hint of salt and knew the sea was close.

Beating my wings, I rose into the dark.

I darted south through the wood towards Dragafjall. Moments later, a faint shimmer of light appeared, first yellow, then red, then orange, then all the colors of the Bifrost swirled overhead in one glorious display. Once it was in sight, I broke through the tree line and headed west, Bifrost above me, the leaf-littered treetops below, barely skimming my feet.

The forest opened up. I could now see Dragafjall's snow-capped fjords. The void of the great sea and the cosmos waited in the distance. As I passed the mountain, the air grew colder. Snowdrifts blew in from the south. The realm of Asgard was now behind me. The stars stretched into the universe, each glittering with the radiance of a diamond. With Bifrost leading the way, I flew past a distant moon and into the cosmos. Flying freely through the universe with gleeful abandon was a moment I always relished.

The farther west I flew, the colder the air became. I would arrive in Jotunheim just before dawn. Below me, I saw the faint outline of the ocean. The colors of the Bifrost disappeared, replaced by ominous greys, signaling giant country was nearing. I dropped toward the sea, passing through misty clouds but never losing sight of the water. Large waves crashed violently onto black sand beaches, leaving behind pure white sea foam and iridescent sea-shells the size of my hands. I flew across the ocean, past the jagged black cliffs and tumbling lava fields, finally reaching a valley floor of tall grasses. I had arrived.

In the distance, the fog lifted, revealing glacial peaks that shone in the darkness like a beacon of light. At the foot of Vestrahorn mountain was the ever-flowing river Iving. Every morning this river led my way toward the shadow forest just on the edge of Jotunheim. A forest named Iron-wood.

After gliding through the cold, thin air, the grasses below me turned to snow, which blanketed the vast landscape. The frozen tundra glittered in the moonlight, speckled with patches of imposing pine trees and large, black, granite boulders. My shadow glided across a frozen lake bordered by evergreens, its surface like a mirror.

An elk looked up as I passed, watching as I dipped below the tree line toward a billow of smoke. Its tanned fur bristled and shook in the breeze as it tipped its antlered head. Just below the smokestack sat a small dwelling. The comforting scent of burning coals and cedar filled my nostrils.

I was home.

With one swooping motion, I landed beside the rock wall that lined the left side of the modest stone dwelling and shifted back into my own shape. Pulling a silver-handled spear from the snow beside the front entrance, I carefully unlatched the iron door handle and stepped in, placing the bloodied spear aside.

Darkness and chilled air greeted me, despite the small fire still burning in the center hearth. My desire stirred. I could already feel Angrboda's warmth radiating from the back room where we slept. After removing my boots so as not to wake her, I carefully made my way across the main living area toward our bedroom. The hearth still glowed with embers which served as the only light in the darkness.

Just past the hearth, I landed one foot into a stack of clay pots. The sound of the pottery breaking echoed loudly through the dwelling.

Shit.

Angrboda's sleepy voice called from the bedroom. "Loki, is that you?"

"No," I reply. "It's Thrym, the ogre."

"Oh good. I could use something different for a change."

"Good to know," I muttered, while continuing toward our bedchamber. Since the arrival of our first child, our relationship had grown a bit stale, which she blamed on the mounting home responsibilities. I suppose I was also guilty of disappearing when such things needed to be tended to, another reason I hoped to someday earn the privilege to move my little family to Asgard with me. (I had a better chance of seeing Odin sing "Underworld Fairie" in a ball gown—a fact Angrboda liked to remind me of.)

In the darkness, I saw the inviting shape of Angrboda as she rolled over in the bed and muttered back, "Please be quiet, you will wake Jormie."

"I wouldn't want to do that." I removed my garments, annoyed that she had our child in the bed with her. Stepping bare-footed onto the fur rug, I took a moment to admire her shape.

As Angrboda turned onto her back, the coverlets fell to her belly, revealing the lovely fullness of her breasts in the moonlight. She brought a finger to her lips, cueing me to be silent.

"You know," I said while lifting the silken covers, "allowing him to sleep in here with us does him no good. He needs to learn to be on his own."

"Why? So he can become a loner like his father?"

"Independent, Angie. He needs to learn how to be independent of us. Teaching him to sleep with us is not helping matters." I gently guided my hand under the cool scales of my child's belly and moved him to the bedside table so I could be next to her.

"Easy for you to give parenting advice, you're never here. He likes this. And where were you last night?"

I paused before speaking. Even I, the most talented liar, was finding it difficult to uphold this facade lately. Angrboda didn't approve of my doings with Odin as much as he wouldn't approve of my intimate relations with her. The distrust between Odin and Angrboda was mutual.

I cleared my throat. "I got caught up with some things in Asgard."

"By things you mean you drank too much and had an orgy with your servants?"

Witches. They know everything.

"That's not exactly what happened. You see, Odin asked me—"

"Odin this and Odin that. I'm growing bored listening to your excuses, Loki. I would be more interested in hearing about an orgy with your servants than another wasted favor for that lying lord of the Æsir."

I let out a long exhale, signaling my dissatisfaction with where this headed. Then I slid into the bed next to Angrboda. My hand found the curve of her hip as I buried my face in her hair and kissed her neck. I inhaled her scent, a blend of vetiver and smoky amber.

"Well then," my lust to have her tugged at me, "perhaps we shouldn't talk at all." I gave her taut bottom a gentle squeeze. "I can't wait to feel you." I ached to be inside of her —she was intoxicating. A torrid and lust-filled affair that started somewhat unexpectedly had been a welcome gift for my sanity, or what was left of it. The gods scorned me for who I was, but Angrboda embraced it.

At least she had then. Now she slept and ate a lot and took care of our child, who was growing unruly. Just last week, we found him taking a piss inside one of her cooking cauldrons. When scolded, the serpent sent me a look of defiance before slithering under the furniture. Sometimes it felt as if my own child hated me, a heartbreaking thought. Angrboda blamed his misbehaviors on my absences, a reality I hated to admit might be true.

I pressed my hips into her backside and kissed her bare

shoulder, hoping she wouldn't resist my advances. "Did you hear me?" I whispered. "Feel what you do to me?"

She took my hand and placed it on her belly. *Lower.* My fingers crept in between her silk thighs searching for her warmth. *There we go, now I can—*

"I'm pregnant."

—vomit.

"*What?*" I spoke too loudly. Jormungandr stirred and let out an irritated hiss.

"Oh see, now you woke him. You don't understand what it is like trying to put this child to sleep."

She flung the covers from her naked shape and began to handle our serpent child, who tried desperately to wriggle away.

Mesmerized, I watched his black scales shine as he flipped and fought in the moonlight that streamed in from the window.

This was the last thing I expected or needed—a complication to my plans.

"Pregnant?"

Angrboda sent me an exhausted look, a look I hated. Her hair, black and wild, fell below her waist in tangles as she chased our firstborn through the bedsheets. "That's what I said."

Jormungandr's tail flicked past me as he broke free from her grasp.

"Loki, grab him please, before he disappears into the hearth again."

"The hearth?" My hands searched for the serpent between the bed sheets.

"Yes. It's a new thing he's gotten into when he's upset. He hides."

"Do you ever think he's just a spoiled brat, Angie? We

shouldn't allow him to do such things unpunished."

The snake's tail appeared beside me as he slithered under the pillows. I grabbed hold of it with one hand. "Gotcha."

"Good, now you handle him, since you are the parenting expert. I am exhausted." She reached for a long, sheer robe and slipped it on. I brought the serpent to my chest as I sat up in the bed to watch her. He curled up in a loop and rested his head so that his yellow eyes faced me.

"Why can't you just behave?" I asked him while petting his angled snout. "The hearth? What has gotten into you?" The serpent's eyes drifted shut and his split tongue lolled from the center of his mouth onto my bare chest. "He grows very fast." I observed the length of our child snout to tail. "Even since just yesterday."

Angrboda made her way back to the bed with a small candle. I watched as she placed it in a tray on the night-stand and lit its wick with magic. "See how good he is for you. It takes me hours to get him to sleep like that." She sat down on the feathered mattress and began to stroke the back of Jormungandr's head.

We interlaced our fingers together and stared at one another in the darkness.

A second child? Was I ready for this? I supposed that was irrelevant; it was coming no matter what.

My eyes traveled to her belly, which radiated life.

"You cannot keep doing this, Loki, splitting your time between Asgard and here. And gods knows what else you are doing in Midgard and the rest of the realms. I need you here—your family, your *growing* family, needs you here."

"I don't go to Midgard often." Partially true.

"Don't lie to me. I know you were the one who created that strife in the middle world just last week."

"Don't I always bring you back something beautiful from there?"

"You mean like the pots you just demolished outside our bedroom door?"

I'd stolen the pots from a trading post along the Midgardian Sea during one of my recent escapades.

"What were they doing scattered on the floor?"

"Jormie likes to play in them." She crossed her arms. Her eyes, like our son's, burned yellow in the darkness and glowed against her pale skin.

"Great, so our treasures are being used as a child's playthings? He has plenty of other toys, why must he use those?" My temperature rose, frustrated that I flew all the way here to argue over toys and parenting styles.

"He likes those. Or he did, whatever is left of them."

"So now you are going to make me feel worse by blaming me for destroying the only toys that our son likes? Perhaps I'm better off not coming here at all!"

Jormungandr lifted his head and hissed at me. Two small fangs appeared and from them a drop of black venom landed on my bare skin. A searing burn shot through me as it singed my flesh.

"Since when does he make poison!" I scooped up the serpent in my hands to place him on Angie's lap.

"He always has— you have just been too busy to notice."

I rubbed my singed flesh. "And he just spat it at his own father."

"He is just a child, Loki. He doesn't know any better."

The serpent closed its mouth and stared at me. I believed differently. He knew exactly what he had done. "Look at his face, he knows. I know that look. It's guilt."

She picked up the snake and stared in his eyes while he writhed in her hands. "Perhaps he does. Perhaps he's angry that his own father doesn't want to be here."

Those words stung. It wasn't true. I did—I just needed more time.

"I never said that. Give him back to me, please." My heart felt hungry to hold him again, perhaps from the guilt over what I had said. She handed him over. His flesh felt cool against my warm skin as he settled back down.

I avoided her eyes, not just embarrassed about my fumble with the pottery, but because somewhere deep inside I knew she was right, and although I hated to admit it, a part of me desired what she asked for, to be more present with my family. And at least it was a segue to fantastic sex.

"Why must we argue so much lately?"

What could I say? That I was torn between wanting godhood and the family I had never planned? I was a terrible father, uncertain of how to become a better one. Was it terrible to want it all?

I ran a hand over Jormungandr's cool scales as I stared at Angie, speechless. I didn't have to answer; she already knew I was torn.

She climbed onto the bed and hugged my hips with her thighs. Her hands traced my chest as I brought one of mine to her belly. Her touch felt like bliss to my troubled mind.

"I don't want to argue," she whispered. "I'm tired of it." She grazed my lips with hers.

I sighed, feeling bad about our argument, too. "I didn't mean to." I stared at her shape in the faint light of dawn, feeling the familiar ache of wanting her. Her robes opened, revealing her beautifully full breasts again and the three scars between them. With a fingertip I touched the raised flesh as her hand did the same to the scars across my mouth.

She leaned forward, and her long hair fell across my bare

chest, tickling me as she kissed my face. She stopped and stared into my eyes. "I don't want any more treasures, Loki, I want the father of my children here, always, where he belongs."

With eyes closed, my hands traced her navel, desperate to feel the life inside that churned with electric warmth.

"This pregnancy," she said, placing her hand against mine, pressing it farther into the softness of her belly. "It's different, I feel it. We need you here, I need you."

"I want you," I whispered as I took hold of her hips to press myself into her.

"Let him sleep a bit." Angrboda stroked the back of Jormungandr's head once before slowly removing herself from me. She disappeared out of the room, leaving just me, my frustrations, and our sleeping serpent son. I was anxious but excited all at once. The idea of another child stirred something inside of me. She was right—this pregnancy was *different*.

I turned my gaze to the small window on my right and watched as the blood red sky of dawn began to bleed out across the frostbitten landscape of Jotunheim. Although Asgard was beautiful with its majestic fjords and leafy green cliffsides littered with waterfalls like ribbons, this place was a wonderworld. A rare beauty, the gem of the universe, a place on the fringe where only the wildest souls could survive, souls like us. It did truly feel like *home.*

I looked down at Jormungandr, curled up in a ring, sleeping soundly. Was fatherhood enough to lure me from my own selfish pursuits?

PART III

AN UNLUCKY JOURNEY

Do not fear the flame. In time it burns us all.
Jotunheim, Land of the Giants—The next morning

I awoke from a deep but short sleep as the sunlight streamed in from the window across my face. My hand felt for Jormungandr on my bare chest, but he was gone. Throwing the covers off, I sat up, continuing to feel around for my child. The dwelling was quiet—not even the sound of the morning kettle or the smell of spices Angie usually burned upon waking.

I dressed and left the bedroom, noticing that the spear and provisions bag Angie used for hunting was also missing. A drum and several magical staffs hung nearby, all crafted by Angrboda herself. As I glided my fingers across the soft skin of the drum, I felt an uneasiness settle over me. For the first time, her going out hunting with our son unsettled me. I knew she was more than capable of holding her own—I once watched in horror as she drove her fingernails into all ten eyes of a troll who tried stealing an elk from her. Still, she was with child, *my child,* and something about this pregnancy worried me.

Pulling on a fur-trimmed cloak I kept there, I stepped outside into the cold Jotunheim morning. Angie would be less than pleased that I went in search of her like an overprotective mother hen, but if I just flew overhead and watched her from a distance it would put my mind at ease.

To my left was a set of Angrboda's fresh prints in the snow, pointing north toward one of the places the big elk roam. I transformed into falcon shape and took to the skies to follow her tracks.

As I flew north, the air grew colder. The skies darkened. My sense of direction scrambled, and my vision clouded. Snow fell at an alarming rate. A crack of thunder startled me along with a blinding flash of lightning. I gasped as the air stifled my breathing. Magic was at play. Not just any magic—it was the kind of magic I was most familiar with, illusion magic. The prints in the snow disappeared as if they had never been there at all.

Because they hadn't been. It was a trick—one meant to trap me.

I banked to the south, desperate to change course unnoticed by the magician searching for me. I glided away from the squalls, but it was too late. A blast of wind plunged me from the sky. There was a ringing in my ears so loud it hurt. Everything blurred as I tumbled to earth.

Just before I hit the ground, a huge hand reached out and grabbed me by the tail. I shook my feathers, attempting to shapeshift, but the grasp tightened, and my magic was useless. The hand turned me over, belly up, and I was greeted by two huge, flaring nostrils and a black, bristled beard framing a wide face.

Thrym, lord of the ogres.

"Gotcha." Thrym's breath stunk of old blood and rotted insects. "And what a fine addition to my stew you shall be." In his other hand he produced a large leather provisions satchel covered with silver buckles and bones hanging from the straps.

"I am not a fine addition to any stew, you idiot, I am—"

Before I could finish my explanation he shoved me head-first into the satchel.

"Loki of Asgard," I mumbled, from between a nest of rotted potatoes and what looked like a rabbit's foot.

The giant didn't hear my pleas. The ground shook as he stalked off with me in the provision bag. Once again, I attempted to shapeshift, but my efforts were useless against a spell he'd used to block my magic. Caught by an ogre for stew—this was a first for me. Angie would have my head if she knew. I yelled my pleas to the giant, but the boom of his footsteps drowned out my cries.

Not long after, the unmistakable sound of a door opening and closing came through the bag and the sound of his footsteps changed.

"Thrym! What have you got here?" said a thunderous voice. It was the voice of a giantess. The bag swung wildly as she took hold of it.

"Just a bird. A bit of a runt, but it will do as a garnish."

Runt? Garnish? The nerve. "I beg your pardon, but I am not to be made a garnish for any stew. I am Loki of Asgard and I demand to be freed immediately!"

"Did you hear something?" asked Thrym.

"Sounded like a mouse nibbling on a breadbasket."

"Or a beetle wiping its jaw clean."

"Or an ant letting loose a bit of gas."

The two brayed like donkeys at the last remark.

My face burned with rage. My feathers strained against the fabric.

"Better let it out, let me have a look see," said the giantess.

The bag was lifted and untied, and I tumbled to the stone floor. My head throbbed as I looked up at the crooked-toothed grin of Thrym. The air stank of burning sage and cedar.

"See," he said. "Not much to him, but I suppose I could use the feathers for something." He plucked one from my tail.

I screamed in falcon form. "You idiot! Listen to me for a moment!"

The ogre picked me up and held me upside down in front of his face. Hot steam blew from his nostrils. I gagged at the scent. The giantess—who had too many heads to count—stood beside him, arms crossed, each pair of eyes studying me intensely.

"Wait a moment, Thrym, there's something peculiar about this bird." She pointed a knotty-knuckled finger and poked me in the neck. "Look at the eyes."

Thrym's face closed in. I wriggled in his hand as his filthy fingernails dug into my rib cage. "What about them?"

"They're green, very unusual."

"Because"—the predicament enraged me—"I'm not a bird, I'm Loki, son of Laufey in bird form!"

Thrym stared at me blankly for a moment before letting

out a resounding laugh. "Loki Laufeyson? The giant who lives in Asgard among the Æsir—well of course you are!"

"Now that we have that settled, can you please let me go so I can return to Asgard unscathed? Or at least in one piece?" One of my bones cracked under the might of his hand.

"Put him down without strangling the poor thing to death, Thrym. Let's ask him some questions."

At least someone showed common sense. The giant released me onto a large wooden table where I perched, shaking my feathers loose.

"Now, what are you doing in Jotunheim, eh?" asked the giantess, all seven pairs of eyebrows raised at once.

I stared back at her, annoyed. "Just stretching my wings a bit. Now, if you don't mind—" My claws slid on the varnished surface of the table as I took a step. The giant stuck out his hand to stop me from slipping off the edge.

"In a snow squall?" asked Thrym. "I know you better than that, trickster. Come on now, tell us what you're doing here and then maybe we'll consider letting you go."

I scowled. The nerve of an ogre to threaten me. "Who are you to question my actions? As I explained, I was stretching my wings. This is my land as much as it is yours." I folded my wings in front of my breastbone and tried to appear larger.

Thrym brought his hand, which was as wide as I was tall, to his face and chuckled. "This is not your land, Loki. From what I understand you are a traitor and a thief. You work for Odin now."

"I work for no one but myself, thank you very much, so if you don't mind, please free me from your spell so I can continue my morning in peace." I tapped a claw impatiently on the table.

The giants looked at one another and then at me. I tried my best to hide my anxiousness, but my tapping claws gave me away.

"Why, Laufeyson, are you nervous about something?" asked the giantess.

I scoffed, "I was just plucked from the sky by paralyzing magic and had my life threatened, so forgive me if I am a bit anxious to be freed."

Thrym snickered again. I knew that laugh and I didn't like it. I needed to escape before the situation escalated. My eyes found the window behind them, over the sink. Before either could say another word, I took off in the air. Freedom would be mine even if it meant hurling myself full speed through a stained glass window. But something grabbed my tail, catapulting me backward and flinging me upside down at Thrym's feet.

"Not so fast, Loki. I have a better idea," he said as the two ogres smiled at each other. "Now that I have you here, there is something I would like to ask of you."

Holding me by my feet, he made his way toward a stone hearth in the center of the dwelling. I gulped as the heat of the roaring fire grew closer. "What is it?" I asked. "I hope it's not what herbs I prefer to be marinated in."

The giantess cackled. "We will be the ones to decide that."

My eyes fixed on the red-hot coals at the bottom of the hearth. I did not want to die as a side dish for giants. "What is it?"

"Just a little favor," said Thrym as he picked his nose with his free hand and brought me closer to the hearth.

"Name it." I was desperate. The heat made me sweat. The giantess appeared beside us with a small pail. I watched as she threw what appeared to be animal parts in the fire. The scent of burning flesh filled the air. I coughed as the grip of the giant tightened.

Thrym turned me so that my eyes faced the embers. "I want the hammer of the god. You know, the one Thor always makes a fuss about, bragging about being a giant killer and all."

"You want Mjolnir?" I fought the urge to laugh. That was ridiculous. *Impossible.* "That's not a little favor." The flames in the hearth continued to eat away at the bones as if they were nothing.

"A small exchange to spare your life." The giant chuckled and moved me closer to the blaze. I was about to become a roasted appetizer for their feast. Stealing Thor's hammer would be no easy feat, and one that would certainly be noticed. But perhaps this could work in my favor.

"Fine. I will bring you the hammer of the gods in nine days." That should give me enough time to cook up an alternate plan.

"Not good enough, trickster. By two sun downs."

"Two sun downs? Are you mad?"

The giant let out a sadistic laugh. "And if you fail to bring me the hammer, I will ensure that all of the nine realms learn of that brood of monsters you are creating here in Jotunheim—especially the witch's husband."

Husband? I looked at the giant. "Did you say husband?"

The giant grinned. "Ah yes, trickster, long before you came around there was another one of your kind meddling with that witch, but a god of Asgard."

Fuming, I shook myself free. "Free me from this spell now and I will grant what you ask of me."

The giant appeared amused. "Did I strike a nerve?"

I was anything but amused as I struggled to process what he'd said. I seethed about Thrym's revelation that

Angrboda had a secret past. "Release me from this spell."

"Very well, trickster." He pressed one large thumb against my forehead. I felt lighter and my headache diminished. I was freed. Taking flight, I darted through the open door and made my way south.

I flew with record speed back to my home in Ironwood, urged on by my rage. I stormed into our dwelling.

Angie looked up at me from the hearth. "By the blade of my spear what are you doing?" She dropped the wooden mortar in her hand onto the floor and brought the other hand to her mouth to stifle a laugh, which further fueled my anger.

I caught a glimpse of myself in the mirror. My copper red hair stood out in all directions, a few remaining feathers poking out. My cloak, partially torn, hung from my shoulders in tangled knots. One foot remained a claw, while the other had returned to its normal fur-trimmed boot. My appearance reflected my inner turmoil, but I didn't give a shit.

I stepped over Jormungandr who slithered across the floor toward the safety of a wooden chest. "A god of Asgard," I thundered. Our son hid as I questioned Angrboda. She had betrayed me, lied to me. It was as if I didn't know her at all. She rolled her eyes and stood gathering her purple skirts, with no sign of remorse.

"Am I to be subjected to you harping on that all day? It was a long time ago. The marriage was annulled. I haven't seen him in years. What's the real reason you're angry? I reckon it's because you are not the only one in this household with secrets." She headed past me toward the bedroom.

Her words stung, perhaps because they were true.

I grabbed her tattooed arm, but she touched a dagger to my neck. "Do not touch me like that. Ever."

My grip softened as I backpedaled from my mistake. "I'm sorry, but I hate that you have hidden things from me."

"And you haven't?" Her eyes traveled the length of my body. "Do you think I don't know of your escapades in Asgard? Or Midgard? Or Vanaheim? Or . . . name a place. Tell me, Loki, how many lovers have you taken in those worlds since I gave birth to your son? Or is it too many to count? I would have better luck counting the stars at night."

She had a point.

She withdrew the cold steel from my skin. "Exactly."

"Please just tell me it wasn't Baldur." I watched her walk away, disappearing into the bedroom. "Perhaps I will find out on my own when I return to Asgard."

Several items flew toward me. I ducked just in time to miss a pointed heeled boot, which I was certain was mine.

"Stop throwing my things about as if they mean nothing." I picked up the boot from the floor. "These were very difficult to find."

She reappeared in the doorway, her eyes aglow with anger. "You always manage to invent yet another reason to return to Asgard, don't you?"

"I didn't invent anything. I was trapped by Thrym the ogre and it was either agree to his terms or be cooked in a cauldron over hot coals. I must deliver the hammer of the gods to Thrym or else—" I was uncertain I wanted to reveal that he knew of us; her anxieties about our relationship becoming public knowledge were already escalating.

"Or else what, Loki?"

"Or else I will be an oath breaker." I had to lie. The last thing I wanted was to encourage her growing worry that the gods would learn of us.

"Why didn't you use the fire magic that you have been putting into practice so diligently? Or your shapeshifting abilities since you are such the expert now?" She tapped her pointy-toed shoe on the stone floor. She clearly knew of the strife I had been creating.

"He had me under some sort of spell." I was ashamed to admit I had been put in such a predicament. "I couldn't use my magic."

"But you had your words, no?" Angrboda walked toward me wielding the dagger again. "I thought you were silver-tongued. That you could negotiate anything with anyone. What happened, Loki?" She crossed her arms and waited for an explanation.

"Don't you see, Ang, there is no way Thor won't notice his hammer is gone. He practically sleeps with it. It's Asgard's most prized treasure and dare I remind you—"

"You tricked the dwarves to craft it for them, I know, Loki, you have told me that story several *hundred* times." She let out an exhausted sigh.

It annoyed me that she disregarded such a feat. "Oh, so now the truth is revealed. I knew you never wanted to hear about that." Her admission that she didn't love my tales about my achievements hurt.

"I didn't want to be rude but after the first twenty times or so, it got a bit repetitious. Yes, if it weren't for you, the gods wouldn't have the treasures. Sif would not have her magical hair and," her angry voice echoed through the walls of the dwelling, "let us not forget to mention, you would not be so bitter from having your mouth sewn shut!"

I gasped, floored that she made light of the worst thing that had ever been done to me.

How dare she?

We stared at one another for a moment in painful silence.

"Well," I finally said, "I suppose it's always a good thing

to know how your partner really feels. I will never make mention of it again. Happy?"

Angie wiped a stream of spittle from her mouth and looked remorseful. She shook her head. "No, Loki, I'm not happy at all. My point is that I don't think it's good for you to get yourself tangled up in their affairs again." She took a step toward me and reached out to run her fingertips along my scars. "No good ever comes from it."

"This time it's different. The gods will never stand for the hammer to go missing. They will do anything to have it returned. Once they notice it's gone, they will commission me to find it and I will negotiate my own terms with Thrym, and with the gods." Pleased with my idea, I folded my arms and rocked back on my heels.

Angie did not look impressed. "I thought you were done with this god nonsense. I thought you were going to stay here with your family and instead off you go to Asgard to become immersed—yet again—in another scandal that you love so much. I'm beginning to believe you just like the attention more than being with me."

She stormed past me towards the window of the hearth room. I needed this plan to work, but I also wanted my family, so I followed her, leaping sideways to avoid the indifferent Jormungandr, who slept in a sunny spot on the stone floor. "Must he just sleep anywhere? I practically stepped on him!"

Angie sent me a look that said this was not a good time to discuss her parenting decisions. "Speaking of being anywhere, why were you out that way?"

I was hesitant to explain.

With one finger, she traced the inscribed runes in the wooden trim of the window.

"Tell me the truth." Her voice had turned gentle.

She was already upset with me, so I had nothing more to lose. "I was looking for you."

"Looking for me?"

"I didn't like the idea of the mother of my children out hunting alone."

To my surprise, her face softened. Perhaps I wasn't the only one beginning to change.

I placed one finger on hers. We traced the rune Berkano together just like we had after the first time we made love, her naked shape still trembling with ecstasy against mine.

"You know I'm more than capable of taking care of myself."

I placed both my hands on her belly as Jormungandr slithered between our feet and wrapped himself around our ankles. "That doesn't mean I don't worry about you." In her eyes I saw love, I saw understanding despite my selfish ways and undeniable flaws. Her eyes traveled to a wound on my arm that I must have received during my squabbles with the giants.

"Let me fix that," she said.

I watched as she gathered various herbs from jars. Mugwort, waybread, lamb's cress, venom-loather, mayweed, crabapple, and fennel. With a wooden pestle, she crushed them into a powder that she mixed with soap and the juice of an apple inside a mortar. Then she boiled it along with a paste made from ashes, fennel, and a beaten egg. Seeing such practices stirred memories of my childhood as I watched my mother work with similar herbs. She was a master with healing magic whom I missed greatly.

Angrboda massaged the resulting salve into my wound and with a soft voice, repeated a short poem.

"Chervil and fennel, two mighty worts.

There the apple did against venom.

May all weeds spring up by their roots.

The seas slip apart, all salt water, when I blow this venom from you."

Angrboda blew air softly over the wound, which closed as if it had never existed. Then she let out a huge sigh. "I swore I would never hold you back, didn't I?"

"You did."

Gently, she took my hand in hers. "I want to show you something. Come here." She led me to a wooden sea chest that sat in the corner of our main living area. Kneeling down beside it, she unlatched its locks and stared up at me. "Before you get angry with me, I moved some of your things to fit this trunk in this spot until we find a suitable place for it."

"Moved?"

Angrboda sighed. "Tossed out."

"Tossed out? As if they were rubbish!"

She blocked me with her arm as I lunged for the chest. "Loki, they were rubbish. You must admit you're a bit of hoarder."

"I don't hoard, I keep things of value."

She raised an eyebrow.

"Sentimental value."

"A ten-year-old bejeweled shoe with no mate is sentimental?"

"Yes, it . . . belonged to a Midgardian king."

With a wave of her hand, she disregarded my argument. "Now, moving on." Lifting the lid of the chest she motioned for me to look inside.

Still bitter from her tossing my things, I hesitated to look. Nothing she showed me would be of more value than my treasures.

"It's not done yet, but it's a start."

A giant stone slab with our names carved in runic lettering sat inside. Behind them was the etching of a serpent and two figures who resembled Angrboda and me.

"Think of it as a start to a family portrait," she said. "Of course, we'll need to add the name of our new little one when it arrives."

I looked at Angrboda in disbelief that she had created such a touching memoir for us. "Ang, it's beautiful."

"Really? I did my best with your image, but we know how . . . vain you can be."

"Vain? I'm not vain." I smoothed a strand of my hair back into place.

Angrboda inclined her head.

"I care about my looks, that's all."

"Loki, you once spent an entire sunrise shadowing your eyes."

"I wanted to look my best."

"You were going to Svartalheim, where it's always dark and the dwarves barely reach your knees. Do you really believe they care or can see how you dress your eyes?"

I straightened my tunic. "It was a crucial negotiation."

Angrboda sighed.

Eager to see her creation, I returned my attention to the stone. "Well, let's get it out, I want to see it."

We reached in and lifted the stone from its place, setting it against the sea chest so it faced the center of the room. We sat beside it and held hands as Jormungandr slithered toward the stone. His tongue slipped out as he found a place to nestle between us.

"Come back soon, promise me that," she said. She slid from her pocket a small straw doll fastened together with ribbon. I had gifted her the doll a long time ago.

"You still have this?" My hand grazed its ribbon. I was

touched by her sentimentality.

"Of course. This was the first gift I had ever received from anyone."

Gently I tipped her chin towards mine. My mouth grazed hers. It was soft and inviting. We kissed once, my hand travelling to the warmth of her belly to feel my unborn child. I took her face in my hands.

"Remember our first night here together?" I asked. "What I promised you?"

She nodded and placed her hands on mine. Her cool fingers glided over my warmed skin, tantalizing my senses. I could feel my fire tugging to have her. "I do, although I believe you were so high on mugwort you would have promised me anything to have me." A smile formed on her perfectly crooked mouth that had pleasured my flesh endlessly so many cold nights.

Retrieving the drum that sat nearby, Angrboda shifted her weight towards me. I opened my arms, welcoming her into my embrace. Hugging her close, my hands travelled to the drum in her lap, which she tapped lightly. The sound soothed my mind as it reverberated through my heart center.

Squeezing her tightly, I whispered my promise again. "I meant it. I will *never* forsake you."

She turned her head over her shoulder. A single tear fell from her eye.

My right hand left the drum. I brushed the tear across her cheek. "Trust me." With parted mouths we kissed. For once I felt complete.

PART IV

LET'S MAKE A DEAL

Lie to everyone; save yourself.
Asgard, Home of the Gods—Moments later

I left for Asgard shortly after, hoping my longer than expected absence would go unnoticed. The midday sun warmed my feathers as I rocketed out of the willows and towards my hall. As I did, I released the spell, and the tunnel hidden by the basalt rock column disappeared. Baldur stood beside my hall as his steed drank from a pool of water. Out of sight, I transformed into my usual shape and rounded the corner, as if I had casually emerged from my rooms. He waved at me with one hand as if he had been waiting for me.

Baldur was supposed to be the god of light and all that was good and pure, a façade he played to perfection. But I knew better. I knew about his shadows, his lies, the darkness that he kept so neatly hidden. He was the first to shake my hand in the hall of the gods when I had first arrived in Asgard, and he was also the first to betray me. I understood it wouldn't be the last time.

I wished the animosity between us was due to jealousy on his part. After all, I did attract quite a bit of attention in Asgard, a reality I shamelessly exploited. But I knew that wasn't the case—his feelings went deeper, not to mention he was also Odin's golden boy who could *never* do wrong, whereas I was to blame for almost everything. If Odin missed his mark with his spear, I was to blame. If a fly ended up in Freya's wine, it was my fault. Everything was my fault, even when it wasn't. Baldur could march his horse into Folkvangr and command it to take a shit in the middle of the feast table and somehow, he would not be blamed. I would be.

I hated him, and the feeling was mutual.

Baldur looked at me with his usual smug smile. "Hello, Loki, fancy meeting you here on this lovely day." A breeze from the nearby falls lifted blond hair from his shoulders. It blew perfectly, sickening me.

Taking a closer look at Baldur's face, however, I noticed something peculiar. The usually fresh-faced god looked weary. His cheeks were drawn, his skin pale. His lids drooped over bloodshot eyes as if he hadn't slept in days. I couldn't stop staring at the deathlike pallor of his face.

"My gods," I said, "what is with your eyes? You look as if you haven't slept in ages."

Baldur's smile faded. "I'm having trouble sleeping."

"Better remedy that, you look awful. Perhaps Idun can help with one of her magic apples. Although by the looks of you, it may not work." From my pocket I pulled out a golden apple and took a bite. Its sweet, honey flavor filled my mouth. Instantly I felt youthful. Extending my hand, I offered it up to the god. "Care for a taste?"

Baldur made a face. "I'll pass."

"Suit yourself." With another bite of the apple, I sat down on a large rock beside my hall. "I suppose you have a reason for being here. I hope it's to justify your irritating existence." I kicked off a boot, then turned it upside down to shake out several pebbles.

I turned to look at Baldur's horse who had sniffed in my direction.

"Don't get too excited, it's a mare. I know how much you like those stallions." He patted the horse on its rear and snickered to himself.

"Funny." I sharpened one of my daggers on the rock beside me. "And very original. I've only been mocked for that incident, oh you know, a few hundred times. So yes, well done." I faked a clap in his direction, dagger held loosely in one hand.

His gaze dropped to the ground. "You look tired. Late night?" He plucked a piece of wheat the color of his hair and stuck it in the corner of his mouth.

What was he getting at?

I felt my upper lip twitch as I watched him chew. His very presence stirred irrational anger inside of me. "Tell me, is your goddess just as tired from screaming my name all night?"

Baldur's face hardened and turned scarlet as he spit the grass out onto the ground. He reached for the grip of the sword at his side. I raised my hands and chuckled. "I'm just kidding. Why are you so jumpy?" After tucking my dagger away, with both hands I pulled the boot back on.

His hand relaxed. "Must everything be a joke to you?"

"Must you never joke at all?" Twirling my dagger, I hopped down from the boulder.

He reached for the reins of his horse as he stepped closer to me. "I saw you," he said, "in falcon form heading toward that shadowed tunnel between the trees on the edge of Asgard. The one below the Bifrost. You have mastered shapeshifting, haven't you? And forged a secret passage no one knows about."

Casually I brushed the dust from my pants. "I don't know what you're talking about. There are many falcons flying about. And please get to the point if you have one. I'm hungry and in need of a nap."

"It was you, Loki. I know it was, and it's not the first time I've seen you disappear through there."

"Baldur," I said sweetly as I fingered the edge of his gold-trimmed tunic. "You watch me so closely, come on now, are you in love with me? Admit it. I saw the ugly gleam of jealousy in your eyes when I disappeared with Freyr that night. Do you wish that it was you?"

He swiped my hand away as his face turned pale white, then pink, then as red as an apple. "Don't be ridiculous, you pervert, I would never."

"Because you know," I leaned back on the rock and sprawled with my legs wide, "there is still a chance."

He scoffed and shook his head, preparing to mount his horse. "You are insane."

"Point being?" I waved my fingers as he guided his horse away. "Have a lovely day."

His horse cantered toward the forest.

"That takes care of that."

Springing up from the rock I went through the front door of my hall, letting it slam shut behind me. I peered out the front window to ensure Baldur was truly gone.

Removing my cloak, I tossed it aside and began to pace the length of my chambers, my mind stirring with ideas about how I could steal Thor's hammer.

Like any full-blooded Jotun, Thrym couldn't be trusted, and his knowledge of Angrboda and my growing family disturbed me. But I could only assume that once the hammer of the gods was discovered missing, the gods would petition yours truly to find it, and then I could barter with the giant and the gods for something that would benefit me.

The rattle of a chariot's wheels interrupted my thoughts. The rune-glittered chariot belonging to the goddess Freya rolled past my window. Her golden hair glowed in the mid-afternoon sunlight, as did the whiskers of the two gigantic cats who pulled it. A boar trotted alongside with a gold saddle strapped to its back.

My mind wandered as I watched her. Wouldn't the desirable goddess of love be the perfect tool for bargaining with a wretched beast such as Thrym? I snickered to myself at the thought of trading Freya in some twisted arrangement to marry the ogre in exchange for the hammer.

Oh, what a sweet deal that would be.

My mind considered all the creative ways I could make that happen.

Focus.

I needed to get the hammer.

Drinking horn in hand, I paced. Could I steal the hammer myself? Sneak into Thor's Hall as a fly? No, that wouldn't work. The hammer was far too heavy for me to lift in insect form.

I took a drink of ale as I pondered more ideas. Perhaps I

could somehow coerce Thor to give it to me. But there had to be a good reason, a *very* good reason. Thor never parted with his hammer.

Taking a seat in front of a mirror, I thought of ways I could convince the thunder god to hand over his most prized possession. I braided my hair, then undid it and braided it again. I drew liner around my eyes as I stared into a mirror while modeling various shapes and sizes of earrings and hair beads made from jewels and gold.

Gold. Gold hair. Hair. Golden hair.

Hair as golden as the sun.

Yes. Sif. Thor's wife, the goddess with the golden hair—well, it was more of a weave now. Silly of me trying to plot a theft when there didn't need to be a theft at all. I wouldn't *steal* Thor's hammer, I would have it *handed over* to me, *willingly,* by none other than Thor's loving but ever-not-so-faithful bride.

I dropped the jewels I held and stood up. Where would I find Sif? She only spent time in two places, the bedroom and the feast hall, because my gods did the woman love to eat. It showed on her hips, a well-fed luxury I enjoyed having in my hands.

I made my way toward the feast hall of the gods on the other side of Asgard. Beside it was a long storage cellar sitting at the right angle and kept at the right temperature to safely store Asgard's finest delicacies. This hall was the farthest from mine, a placement I was certain Odin did on purpose due to my hedonism. I had won almost every eating contest the gods had ever put on and still managed to polish off an entire row of sweets afterward.

The low-lying cellar was made of a special stone that never aged, and the roof was layered with moss and straw to dampen the effects of Asgard's plentiful sunshine. At its entrance stood a large oak door with an iron handle. Just outside the door, cropping a patch of strawberries, was Sif's horse, a huge, black and white, spotted stallion with hooves like anvils and thick muscular legs.

Carefully, I stepped around the stallion and down the stairs, which led to the cellar's door. I pushed through the door without a knock and found Sif sucking down a bottle of goat's milk, its bottom tipped toward the ceiling.

I stood for a moment admiring the white liquid spilling down the goddess's breasts, exposed in her revealing gown.

She spotted me and lowered the bottle with a gasp. "What in the nine realms are you doing in here, you little pervert? Shouldn't you be trying on dresses with Idun or whatever it is that you do when you are lurking about Asgard?"

"I suppose I don't need to ask you the same." I pointed to the stains down her bejeweled dress. "You know goat's milk is supposed to be an excellent source of vitamins for your hair . . ." I paused and brought my fingers to my mouth. "Oops. I suppose it doesn't work for weaves. I have enough dresses; I came to speak to you."

Sif narrowed her eyes. "What do you want? I don't have time for your games."

"Very well then." I picked up an apple from a table by the door, produced one of my daggers, and began to slice into its flesh. "I suppose I'll have to ask someone else to help Thor." Placing a slice of apple in my mouth, I waited for Sif's reaction.

Sif's brow furrowed. "What do you mean, help Thor?"

"Oh nothing, never mind. It's just the hammer of the gods. I'm sure we could always have a new one crafted, or . . . go without it. We could always use swords and spears to fight invading giants, and Thor, well, he will just have to learn to live without it. Perhaps I will lend him one of my daggers, or a steak knife." I knew my mention of Thor doing without a hammer was like expecting a puppy to live without its favorite chew toy—*impossible.*

Sif's expression changed from annoyed to concerned to interested.

"What are you talking about?"

"You aren't interested in my *games.*" I opened the door with one hand. "I'll just be on my—"

The goddess moved with surprising agility next to me, shoving one knee between my legs to pin me against the door. She brought a nearby cheese slicing knife to my throat as the dagger I held fell to the floor along with the apple.

"Why, Sif." I was amused at her pitiful weapon and shamelessly aroused. "I know you like it rough but just give me a moment to—"

"Tell me why you speak of Mjolnir in such a way." The dull edge of the knife slid across my skin.

"I was just going to suggest a gift for Thor. But if you're not keen on it, then pretend I never mentioned it."

"A gift?" Her eyes narrowed. The blade pressed harder against my skin. "Since when are you so giving?"

"You should know I can be quite giving when needed." I referred to our taboo night of passion.

The goddess huffed and retreated. "Explain, if it gets you away from me any faster."

Straightening my tunic, I prepared my lies. "You see, when I had the hammer of the gods crafted, remember that time I—"

"Yes, Loki, we all remember the time you tricked the dwarves into making the treasures of the gods, by Odin's beard *must* I be subjected to hearing about it again?"

What was it with these people? Did no one like to hear about my escapades?

"Well, since nothing interesting around here happens unless I instigate it, I figured you would enjoy listening, but I digress. And remember, without *me* you would not have . . ." Running my fingers through my hair, I remind her of the bargain I made with the dwarves for the eternally golden weave that adorned her crown.

Sif let out a loud huff and tapped a finger on the wooden shelf beside her, indicating impatience with my mentioning how I took her hair after our night of passion. A bittersweet memory, at least for me.

"Let's not rehash old times. I neglected to mention the hammer needs *resurfacing* on occasion." I cleared my throat. "Service, if you will."

Her brow furrowed in concentration. She paused a moment; something must have been going on behind those vacant blue eyes.

"Resurfacing?" She raised an eyebrow. "A magic hammer needs resurfacing, do I look like a fool?"

I eyed the patches of milk on her dress and the crumbs splattered across it. "At the moment you look—"

"Watch your words with me, Laufeyson."

"Delicious, I was going to say *delicious.*"

Sif crossed her arms. "If you don't want to end up as part of the charcuterie plate for tonight's feast you will tell me the entire truth. I don't trust you."

"That breaks my heart, after all that we shared."

"You lied to me and cut off my hair. We share nothing but grief."

"I beg to differ. Shall I remind you about how you *begged* me for—"

"Enough!" Her voice pierced my ears as she slammed a

shaking fist on the table beside her. I felt bad for a moment. But it passed.

Maybe fatherhood was softening me.

We stared at one another in awkward silence as the afternoon light shone through the small windows of the cellar.

"I can't trust you, Loki, so whatever it is that you are trying to trick or con or lure me into, it won't work."

"Very well then, I am sure that speck of rust won't grow —for a few years at least."

"Rust?"

"You didn't see it? I wouldn't expect you to. It's very small and possibly harmless. Until a drop of rain gets it, although the likelihood of that is slim, unless Thor summons a touch of rain, which on second thought he does all the time." She looked intent. My plan was working. I could sense she was beginning to worry. "Alas, you don't believe me. Forget my idea, you could always get him a new set of shoes or something. He likes that sort of thing."

Different expressions chased each other across her face. "Rust? If Thor knows of this he will—"

"I know." It was time to look my most convincing. I placed my hands on her shoulders. "That is why we must fix it before he notices. I can't think of a better gift for your husband than to have his favorite thing in all the nine realms shined up like new. That is why I came to you, Sif. You are the only one who can help me do this for him."

She lowered her eyes to my hands. I let go and cleared my throat.

"How will I get you the hammer? It's never out of his sight except when he sleeps."

This was the easy part.

"There is a feast tonight, correct?"

Sif nodded.

"Thor will overindulge in the ale. You can bring me the hammer while he's passed out, and I *promise* I will have it back by the first light of dawn. Just like new. He will never know it was missing. I promise."

One unique feature about Thor's hammer was that it could shrink down small enough to fit into a pocket, which was helpful considering how heavy it was. The thought of heaving that thing across Bifrost all the way to Jotunheim in falcon form was less than appealing.

Thor and Sif lived in the hall known as Bilskirnir, not too far from Valhalla. Tucked up out of sight in the shadows of a garden wall outside of their home, I waited at our agreed upon time. Sif emerged from the side door holding a black satchel tied with a magical string. She handed it to me as I guided her against the wall, which was wrapped in flowered creeper vines.

"What are you doing?" she whispered as I pressed against her.

"What does it look like I am doing? Keeping us in the dark where no one can see us." I found the outline of her mouth in the shadows. "Since we're here," I began, hopefully.

Her hand stung my face. The satchel fell to the ground between my feet.

"I am not interested in entertaining you again. You have slept with every goddess from here to Vanaheim."

Not all. There was one—Sigyn. Who for some reason caused me to fumble like a poorly trained servant.

"You must have misread my intentions." I retrieved the satchel and rubbed my stinging face, although my ego was more bruised than my cheek.

"Are you trying to trick me?" Sif's hair glowed in the moonlight, falling in loose waves to her hips.

"What? Trick? No. Never. That was yesterday's Loki. I have changed my ways." My eyes scanned the darkness as snores from the thunder god rang out from the hall into the night air like a boulder rolling through a minefield.

"Like a snake shedding its skin." Sif looked at me with suspicion. "I don't understand why Thor subjects himself to your company for days on end. But nevertheless, he calls you a friend and I have little choice but to honor that."

"Thor calls me his friend?" It surprised me that he made mention of that to anyone else, considering my reputation. I tried hard to ignore the guilt that rose inside, a twisted knot that settled in my stomach, deep and aching. This was a temporary loss; he would regain the hammer with my help. "Never mind all that, I was never one for sentiment."

"True."

For a moment I felt as if I should apologize to her. But I shook the feeling loose. I had a plan to complete. Thankfully, Sif broke the uncomfortable silence. Her voice was cold and hard.

"Get the hammer fixed like you promised and be back before dawn or I will tell Thor you stole it."

That was more like it. She bundled up the bottom of her sleeping gown and picked her way through the grass to the stone path that led to the doorway of their hall. With hammer in hand and ego displaced, I left for Jotunheim to find Thrym and deliver what I'd promised.

The exchange with Thrym went quickly. To my relief, I appeased the giant by holding up my end of the bargain, though I knew I'd be back soon to barter for its return. At least I was confident my strange little family was safe for now.

After successfully evading Thrym's oven, I returned to my hall in Asgard. After flying back and forth through the snow of giant country, I needed a nap.

The moment I closed my eyes, a sound boomed through my front door followed by heavy, deliberate footsteps. I sat up to find one of Odin's ravens perched on my windowsill. Munin cackled as if he were amused.

"Why you little—" The second I planted my feet on the bare wooden floor, my entire hall shook. Another loud boom joined the cackling. A cloud of sawdust filled my chambers. I about-faced to see the huge silhouette of Thor standing in my doorway in a cloud of dust. Behind him I could make out the remains of my door, splintered to pieces.

"My door!" I exclaimed, infuriated. "That's the seventh door of mine you have destroyed. I will have you know that is custom made from Svartalheim by—" The god's eyes came in view, a bright shocking blue. Small flecks of lightning flashed from his eyelids. Thunder crackled in the distance as Thor took his first steps toward me.

"Never mind the door, I can barter for another." I stumbled backward, knocking into a vase, which crashed to the floor.

The god followed with deliberate footsteps as I scurried around the room until he eventually cornered me atop a sea chest.

"Something wrong?" I asked, trembling. I debated transforming into an insect and slipping into the chest to evade his fury, but I was afraid he would just crush my entire hall until he found me.

Thor growled. His red beard bristled. Streaks of lightning traveled in and out of his fists, which were clenched at his sides. "My hammer, Loki. Where is my hammer?"

I gulped. "What hammer?" I quickly realized that was a terrible choice of words.

With a roar that knocked me sideways, Thor raised a fist. Using illusion, I disappeared and reappeared across the room just in time to see his hand land in the center of my favorite chest and crush it to pieces. All manner of items —amber, jewelry, talismans, a round gold disc—scattered across floor. I had to summon all my strength not to dive for my beloved treasures, some now unrecognizable from the force of Thor's blow.

That could have been me.

After a few seconds of confusion about my location, the god turned to where I stood. He appeared even more infuriated by my trick.

"Sorry, it's just a habit when my life is threatened," I said.

I bolted sideways but he met my strides with just two footsteps and took hold of me by the collar.

"Wait a moment!" He dragged me through the shrapnel of what was once my door. "Just wait a moment!"

The god took me outside and pinned me against a stone wall without a word. I closed my right eye to block out the excruciating brightness of dawn's first light as it peeked over the mountaintops. Baldur arrived to stand next to Thor, sickeningly radiant as always.

Thor's huge hand closed around my neck and I struggled to breathe. Soon I'd be nothing more than a pile of broken bones left to rot outside my own hall. I looked into Thor's eyes, which remained a shocking electric blue as if lightning could shoot out from his pupils and obliterate me.

"Where is my hammer, Loki? It's missing, and you know where it is. I can see it in your eyes. I want my hammer back. Now." His hand squeezed again, my neck like a twig in his huge fist. I gasped for air as his grip tightened.

"I knew you were up to something last night." Baldur poked a finger into my chest. "I should have known better than to let you be."

"That," I choked out between labored breaths, "was just my normal look."

"There is nothing normal about you." Heimdall had appeared. Of course he would show up to see the spectacle. "Tell us where the hammer of the gods is, or I will make you." He shoved the sharp end of his sword near my privates. "Well?"

Thor eased his grip enough for me to speak.

"What leads you to believe this is my fault?" Sif could have come clean about our exchange, but I doubted it. She wouldn't risk admitting she had trusted me.

"Everything is always your fault," said Baldur.

"Have you checked your goats?" I directed the question to Thor. "They do eat everything."

Thor growled. The dawn's light set fire to his red beard. His eyes burned brighter, and although he was one of my very few friends here, his allegiance to his precious hammer outdid his loyalty to me.

"Do you really think I would steal the hammer of the gods? I would have to be insane to do such a thing." I shook, afraid I wouldn't live to see the light of the next day.

"Last time I checked, you *are* insane," said Heimdall. The wings of his gold helmet tipped back and forth as he spoke.

"Your helmet is crooked."

Heimdall grunted, attempting to adjust the golden gear adorning his abnormally large head. It tilted sideways as Baldur directed him on how to straighten it. I chuckled to myself.

"Is something funny, trickster?" Heimdall asked. "Or should I call you the god of nothing?"

I hid my anger at his remark, but my blood began to boil.

"He is the god of something," said Baldur, "lies. And that's all he will ever be."

That one burned. "I would rather be a god who tells lies than a god who lives one. Your brother may be blind, but you're the one who can't see."

"What does that mean?" he asked.

"Blind to the lies you tell yourself. You're not all light, Baldur."

The color from Baldur's face drained. His brow creased. "I think you seem to forget who was the first one to welcome you to Asgard, Loki."

"That was a long time ago."

Thor grunted. "Stop bickering. Loki, I want my hammer back. *Find it.*"

Thor let go of me with his version of a gentle shove and I tumbled backwards. Once I regained my composure, I straightened my clothing and faced the three gods.

"Of course." I began to walk toward my hall. "I will just see myself off now in search for it."

"Won't you need Freya's cloak?" asked Heimdall with a smirk.

I paused. "Pardon?"

Baldur chimed in next. "Freya's feathered cloak. How else do you expect to fly about the realms looking for it? Transform into a falcon?" He folded his arms across his chest as he awaited my answer.

"You're right. Silly me."

"Folkvangr is that way." Heimdall pointed north in the direction of Freya's home.

Changing course, I said, "I suppose I'll be off to Sessrumnir to ask the goddess if I may borrow it."

The gods watched me walk in the direction of Freya's Hall. I turned back once. Baldur waved with a smile as Thor looked as miserable as a god could.

Moments later, I arrived at Freya's home. I found her in a high ceiling room where she practiced magic. In the center was a set of gold stairs and at the very top was a large open window. Beside the window was a platform in which the goddess could take flight from with her special cloak called Fjathrhamr. Freya was at the top of the stairs kneeling on a large golden chair that faced the platform. In one hand she held a wand made of deer antler and in the other a feather.

I stood at the bottom of the stairs and watched as Freya rocked gently in a trance-like state. With a circling of her wand, she began to transform into a falcon. Her hair, which was spun in braids, slowly turned into fine, iridescent fibers. The fibers grew together, and their centers formed a vein. Around the vein formed the makings of a feather. First it was one, then two, then a hundred or more. Next, her shoulder transformed in the same manner. Flesh turned to feather. Each fiber spun and then straightened until her entire arm was a wing.

Extending the wing, she lifted her other arm. The feathers stretched and expanded, each barb within them glittering in the sunlight. She repeated her charms once again but this time instead of continuing to shapeshift, her feathers shifted back to hair and skin. She muttered a curse word and dropped the wand at her feet. It rolled down the stairs, stopping at the tip of my boot. I picked it up and studied the runes inscribed on it. Freya, still unaware of my presence, let out a heavy sigh and rubbed her forehead, indifferent about her dropped wand.

"Still can't quite master falcon form, I see." My words

echoed from the tall ceiling. How it burned not to tell her that I had, but I couldn't. If the gods knew I had mastered the dangerous art of shapeshifting I would be watched even more than I was now.

Gathering her skirts, Freya stood and spun around to face me. "What are you doing in here?" She was breathless. Her face was red and glistened with sweat. "Haven't I told you that I don't want you in my hall anymore?"

The goddess stormed down the stairs, her movements clumsy, perhaps still disturbed at her failure. She reached for a glass on a nearby table and took a long drink.

I pulled out a chair and motioned for her to sit. "Relax for a moment."

With her upper lip curled, she sat. One of her cats, a grey long-haired beast, emerged from an opened chest and slunk towards us. As he paced past me he arched his back and hissed.

"Even my cats don't like you." Freya began to undo an herb bundle in a dish on the table. "What do you want, Loki, besides interrupting my magical practice?"

"Is that what that was?"

The goddess raised an eyebrow and by the look on her face, I knew I skated on thin ice.

"You have one minute of my time and one only."

"I need to borrow—"

"No."

"You didn't even allow me to finish what I—"

"I don't need to. Whatever it is, the answer is no." She dropped the herb bundle and stared at me. "Must I remind you that the last time I let you borrow anything of mine you returned it in tattered pieces?"

"That dress looked better tattered in my opinion."

"It was my favorite dress."

"And I returned it. As promised."

"In pieces."

Clearly this was getting nowhere. I needed to take a different approach to gain her favor. "Thor's hammer has been stolen."

The goddess stood, knocking the chair over. "What?"

"I know, I know, terrible thing indeed, anyway—"

"Who would do such a thing?"

"I don't know," I spoke quickly, "and there's no sense in discussing it now."

"We need to find it, immediately. All of Asgard is in danger, the nine realms even."

"Which brings me to why I'm here. May I borrow your feathered cloak, so I can find the hammer?"

Freya paced the room. I fiddled with the hem of my tunic, anxious for her answer. She stopped beside a row of staffs, which hung on the wall beside a large bookcase. She pointed a sharp finger my way. "Is this some sort of trick?"

"Trick? Me? No. Never."

"You seemed to have no trouble taking bird form when sneaking about my chambers. Why the sudden need for my cloak?"

I cleared my throat, preparing the lies. "Small birds, bluebirds, sparrows, a jay here or there, yes. Larger birds I haven't quite mastered. I may never. You know how difficult it is. And if I am to be soaring all over the nine realms in search of this thief, I need to take the most agile and fastest form there is, which means, I need your cloak."

"I see." Freya reached for a staff. She approached me and brought its spear-like end to my neck, its sharp steel edges cold against my skin. "If you are lying to me, Loki, if I even hear of one lie being told—anything about this—I will cut you to pieces and feed you to my cats, and whatever they don't finish will be sent to Nidhogg the corpse eater, do you understand?"

My eyes traveled to the grey beast, which grumbled low in his chest in agreement. "You have my word."

With a nod, Freya made her way over to a tall chest. She opened its doors and retrieved her feather cloak.

"Before I give this to you," she reached for a jar, "I'm going to perform a spell that will help you find this thief." She undid its lid and removed three items: a sprig of thorn bush, a piece of wood, and a small bronze pin hammer. She placed the items neatly on the table, one by one. With a small knife she carved the small piece of wood into a stave with two dots representing eyes and a line separating them. In the right eye she placed the pin and spoke the words, *"In Buskan Lucanus."* I watched with curiosity, always awed by the magic the Vanir goddess performed.

She lifted the piece of wood and the hammer. "I will place this outside of Thor's Hall." Then she handed me the sprig of thorn bush. "Take this and keep it on your person at all times." I placed the sprig into a small leather pouch on my belt; then she handed me the feather cloak. "Please take care of this. It took me a long time to perfect."

Fastening the magical cloak to my shoulders, I readied myself to climb the stairs to her platform to take flight. Before spreading my arms to enter the sky, I turned back to Freya. "Why did you defend me?"

The goddess inclined her head. "What do you mean?"

"In Odin's Hall. When I first arrived in Asgard you defended my idea to build walls around Asgard when Heimdall mocked me. Why?"

"Because I understand what it means to make a sacrifice for the betterment of all. Even if that means sacrificing your dignity."

I looked at Freya. No words were spoken; none were needed. Though I doubted we would change much in our interactions, we may have begun to understand each other. And with that I leapt from the platform into the clouds to make my way to Jotunheim.

With the help of Freya's feather cloak, I flew back to Jotunheim as swiftly as I ever had before. But to complicate my journey, it was the coldest day I'd ever experienced. Snow squalls blew from the north, making visibility poor. With the help of magic to navigate, I arrived at Thrym's great hall a little before noon in the ice-cold realm, exhausted and low on patience. The giant sat atop a large rock pile with his feet buried in the snow. As I approached, he wiped his hands clean after picking his teeth with a finger and flicking whatever it was that he retrieved in my direction.

"Why, Loki," he said with a chuckle. "What brings you back so soon? You look weary. What news do you have for me from Asgard?" The giant raised one huge black eyebrow and I began to suspect Thrym had his own agenda.

"Funny you should mention that, not good news."

The giant chuckled again as he set down a shovel as tall as me. "Did the gods of Asgard send you to bargain for the hammer?"

"You didn't really believe they would just let this go, did you?"

"Of course not, Loki, I was counting on it."

"So was I."

The giant's expression changed. "I suppose I can dig it up —for a fair price, of course."

"Name it." I wanted this over fast.

The giant pointed a finger at the sky. "I am tired of the lack of sun in this realm. These dismal days are getting to me. I want the sun."

The sun?

"And the moon to light the night."

The moon?

I had finally found a Jotun more insane than myself. I had tried that once before with terrible consequences. It was highly unlikely they would trust my counsel again. I had to convince him of something else, something more desirable, something . . . *Desire*. Yes, perhaps the goddess of such things.

"Mighty Thrym, the gods will not be willing to negotiate such terms. Let us discuss something a bit more feasible, something they will not need to pluck from the sky, something they can do without . . . or *someone*."

"They almost gave it away before, didn't they?" the giant snickered. "A deal you saved them from."

"Yes, I recall that, vaguely." I was desperate to change the topic. "Now, how about we discuss something more likely. I would hate to see you disappointed and without joy. There must be something else that can provide you with the comfort and beauty you seek. What about a," I pretended to think for a moment, "a lover, or better yet, a *wife?*" I flapped the sides of the cloak gently, just enough so that a waft of its scent would reach Thrym's nose.

"What do I smell?" Thrym asked.

"That," I said while stroking the feathers on the cloak, their softness gliding between my fingers, "is Freya, the goddess of love. This is her cloak. She let me borrow it to come here in hopes you would be cooperative."

Thrym's eyes widened. "She did?"

Just as I had planned, mentioning the goddess piqued his interest. I twirled around, allowing the tips of the cloak to graze his monstrous nose. "Oh yes she did. In fact she may have mentioned a special recompense—if you are agreeable, of course."

Again, the giant sniffed the air and as he did, his blood-shot eyes grew wide. "Is she as beautiful as they say?"

"She is," I said eagerly. "Her beauty can light up an entire realm with only one glance. She would put the sun, the moon, and the stars to shame. And her benevolence knows no boundaries. In fact, she graciously lent me her feather cloak just to fly here today." The thought of her spear on my throat as she threatened to turn me into cat food came to mind. Gracious was not a word I usually applied to her.

"Aye," said the giant. He rubbed his chin thoughtfully. "But beauty fades. The strength of Mjolnir does not." He tossed aside his shovel. I sensed I was losing his interest.

"No, no, it doesn't. Not for Freya, not for any of the god-desses. They have the apples of immortality, and a goddess as vain as Freya will never venture from Asgard without them. No, mighty Thrym, Freya's beauty will never fade." I leaned in to whisper the next part. "Nor will her lustful ways. And I heard she likes it *every* which way."

The giant grinned. "I want her," he said. "Bring me Freya and you may have the hammer back."

Bingo.

Right where I wanted him.

PART V

THOR'S WEDDING DAY

The fox condemns the trap, not himself.
Asgard – Jotunheim—Later that day

E nlivened, I arrived back in Asgard to explain what
Thrym wanted in exchange for the return of Mjolnir
and found Thor pacing in front of my hall.

"Have you just been waiting here the whole time for me
like—"

Thor grabbed me by the collar and shook me hard.
"Where is it? Tell me where my hammer is, Loki. Tell me

now!" My feet left the ground as the thunder god lifted me over his head.

"Put me down and I will tell you everything. I don't appreciate you manhandling me like I'm some sort of dog."

Thor let go, his chest heaving from the stress of losing his beloved weapon. I watched with concern as two feathers fell from Freya's cloak.

"Take a deep breath, I found your hammer. Thrym has it."

"Thrym the ogre? How did he—"

"Never mind that. He has it and he's willing to return it for a price."

Thor stared at me. "But I don't understand how a giant could have gotten my hammer." Thor's eyes searched the ground as if the answers were there.

"I don't know, perhaps you lost sight of it when you were drunk." I put a hand on his broad back and leaned in to whisper my next words. "Don't worry, Thor, I won't make mention of your carelessness to Odin, or any of the gods for that matter. Your secret is safe with me."

Thor's eyes quickly turned to me. "This is your doing." A fair accusation considering how well he knew me.

"My doing?" I scoffed. "Didn't we already discuss this? Do you really believe I have nothing better to do than steal your hammer and give it to a giant just to create strife in Asgard? I have better things to do with my time."

"It's suspicious, Loki. I don't trust you."

I rubbed my forehead. "No, it's *exhausting*. I just flew all the way to Jotunheim, traveled for hours with nothing to eat or drink, journeyed across the entire realm in a snow squall through heavy winds and hail with aching limbs and a headache that has grown worse by the moment to find *your* hammer, and this is the gratitude you show me? Fine.

You can go to Jotunheim and barter for your precious hammer. I am done here." I turned towards my door, which was still split in half.

Thor appeared indifferent to my troubles. "I will go to Jotunheim, find Thrym and crush him with—"

"With what?" I asked. "Your hands?"

Thor grunted. "What does he want?"

"Freya. He wants Freya."

"Oh," replied Thor.

I allowed Thor time to process what I had said.

"For?" he asked.

"To eat."

Thor pondered my response. "An ogre cannot eat a goddess!"

I took a deep breath, wondering how I had possessed the patience for Thor all these years.

"I know, you idiot, he wants to marry her."

"Oh," said Thor. "That should be simple enough. The gods of Asgard will do anything to get my hammer back. We need that hammer. Let's call a counsel of the gods and demand that Freya submit to Thrym's wishes."

The gods and goddesses assembled quickly in the main hall. Thor and I stood inside its front doors as we waited to speak, while all attendees glared and whispered in my direction.

I scanned the room. My eyes landed on Odin who sat in his high seat. Beside him was his daughter, Sigyn, a shield maiden and goddess who I was fond of. When I first arrived in Asgard I witnessed her defy all odds and win a target throw with a sword fit for a king. She was stronger than most gods, outspoken, and lucky for me, a friend.

Perched on the armrests of Odin's chair were his two

ravens Hugin and Munin. His wolves Geri and Freki paced the room, playfully chasing after Freya's cats, who couldn't be bothered.

As I observed the leers and whispers, Freyr's gigantic golden bristled boar Gullinbursti trotted over to greet me. The beast looked up from under a mop of glowing hair as I scratched his ears. He snorted in approval before moving on to investigate a spilled apple that rolled across the marbled floor nearby.

"Let me do the talking," I said to Thor, who already had a haunch of meat in his left hand.

The god took a huge bite and swallowed before letting out a belch. He turned to me and smiled.

"Did you even chew?" I asked.

"What for?" Thor looked towards the table which held the food.

"Never mind."

From the far corner of the room was his wife, Sif, who was watching me with a nervous expression. I left Thor to the food for the center of the room to address the gods, purposefully taking the long way so I could approach Sif. As I passed where she stood, I whispered, "It can be another one of our little secrets."

She mouthed the words *I hate you*, but I didn't care. With her hands out, Freya approached me.

"My cloak," she said with ice in her eyes.

"Of course." I gently removed the cloak and handed it to her, hoping she wouldn't notice the missing feathers.

She took it eagerly and began to inspect its integrity. "What have you done?" she said between taut lips.

"Fixed the problem, as usual," I replied. "Now, allow me to address the hall. Everyone is waiting."

The hall fell silent as I hurriedly pranced into the center

of the room, sending a wave of my fingers to the furious Freya who appeared to have found the damage to her cloak. Propped up beside her now was a long-handled staff which held a ruby amulet on its spear-like end.

Freya looked around the room at the other gods and goddesses before speaking.

"Can we please get on with this quickly? I have better things to do than to listen to this idiot speak," said Freya. "Like clean my cat's litter box."

"Yes, Freya," I said, "you do." I was eager to reveal what Thrym wanted and even more eager to see her reaction, even if it was the last thing I ever would see.

Odin, the highest of all the gods and treacherous brother of yours truly, tapped his spear on the floor of the hall to signal silence. "Tell us, Loki, why have you and Thor summoned us here?"

The voice of Heimdall rang out across the hall. "I hope it's to explain why you are wearing womanly makeup." Several of the gods chuckled.

"We all know why I wear this. It's what you prefer."

Heimdall's face grew scarlet. He opened his mouth to speak but Sigyn interrupted.

"Allow Loki to speak."

The room fell silent upon her command. Sigyn smoothed her royal blue dress before taking a seat beside Odin. She inclined her head as a signal for me to continue.

"Thank you," I began. "And no, I'm not here to discuss my beauty secrets—my apologies to Freya, but I can share those with you at a later time."

Freya narrowed her eyes and tapped her bejeweled fingers while I continued to address the gods. "As you are all aware, the hammer of the gods went missing." My eyes traveled to Freya, who sat filing her nails. "And I, Loki, journeyed far and wide to find it and am pleased to announce I have discovered the culprit and was able to barter for its return. You can all thank me later."

The gods and goddesses began to whisper again. Freya locked eyes with me. As if she already knew where this was going. The excitement coiled in my stomach.

"Tell us where the hammer is," said Odin, "and the price we must pay to get it back. We will do anything."

Perfect. "That is *exactly* what I hoped you would say." I winked at the golden goddess. "Thrym, lord of all the ogres has it, and he wants the hand in marriage of the beautiful Freya as payment, if she obliges, of course."

"You snake!" Freya's eyes turned black as she picked up a spear from beside the table and hurled it at me.

The goddess charged across the room, red-faced and shaking. I ducked behind Thor. Runes spilled out in all directions from her closed hands as she conjured them. She reached for her long-handled staff.

I was in for it.

"I know you had your hand in this, you pervert! I should have never lent my cloak to you!"

Thor stepped aside as Freya opened her hands, sending a rune spell in my direction.

I cast an illusion, disappearing from where I stood and reappearing on the other side of the room, next to Odin.

"You and your cowardly illusion magic! If any of you think for one moment that I am going to Jotunheim to marry that ogre just to get a hammer back, you are all insane!"

Thor refused to let anyone speak of his hammer that way. "It's not just a hammer." The sound of thunder rumbled throughout the hall. Infuriated, he lifted the table, spilling its contents on the floor, including the box which held the Apples of Immortality.

Gullinbursti trotted over to vacuum up the spilled food with his monstrous snout. Odin's wolves scampered to join in the scavenger hunt for spilled delicacies. Idun, the goddess who guarded the apples, rushed to rescue the precious fruits from being devoured by the beasts.

Freya could implode the hall from the inside out if she wanted to. Even Odin was no match for her magic; the gods were right to be frightened. I cowered beside Odin's seat, attempting to hide my delighted laughter as the gods and goddesses began a verbal battle, while Freya and Thor argued over his unhealthy attachment to Mjolnir. The only one who remained silent was the guilty Sif. Even the usually demure Freyr was now shouting for Thor to agree. The hall was in chaos, and I loved every second of it.

A golden apple rolled past. Quickly I stopped it with the tip of my boot and snatched it up for a bite.

Heimdall spoke loudly over the fray. "I say we allow the one at fault for this calamity to be the one who fixes it."

Of course, everyone turned to me, including Thor, who was fuming at Freya's refusal to put on a bridal crown.

"Wouldn't that be Thor?" I asked while stuffing the remaining apple in my pocket. "Considering it is his hammer and all, and his carelessness in letting it go missing." The thunder god sent me a death stare. He stormed toward me, yanking me out from behind Odin.

"How dare you." He shook me, his eyes aglow with electricity.

"Will you stop shaking me and let me think here for a moment?" I pleaded. "And you," I said to Heimdall. "If you know everything, why don't you suggest an alternative?"

Heimdall grinned. "I think," he began. "We should dress Thor as a bride and send him to Jotunheim in Freya's place."

Gullinbursti snorted. Odin's wolves howled. The two ravens Hugin and Munin cackled and croaked as the gods all chimed in to agree to Heimdall's idea.

Only one god disagreed. Thor let go of me and I scuttled back behind the throne.

"Absolutely not," he said. "I do not wear women's clothing. Why don't you send Loki? He is the one that likes that sort of thing."

Thor continued to protest, but everyone was already in agreement that this would be the best solution, and I grew more satisfied with the situation than I could have possibly imagined. Even Sif agreed this would be the only way.

The mighty thunder god Thor in a wedding gown? Why, that was pure brilliance. The debate continued amongst Thor and the other gods and goddesses. All but the god Bragi, the skaldic god of poetry, who stepped into the center of the hall with his lute. Not fond of Bragi's lute playing, I cringed at the first strum, which was followed by a song:

"Loki Laufey-son, the trickster in disguise
Thor Odin-son, the god with lightning in his eyes
The hammer of the gods is gone
Stolen by a thief who may be all brawn
Now the giants will invade Asgard
With ill intent they come
And will shed blood with no regard
Unless Thor Odin-son puts on a bridal crown
And takes with him silver-tongued Loki in a gown
Loki Laufey-son, the—"

Luckily, Heimdall's voice interrupted the tuneful Bragi. "All in favor of voting that Thor puts on a bridal crown?" The gods and goddesses all raised their hands, except for Thor, who looked as if he were about to conjure a storm so large, it would destroy this hall and the ground below it.

I emerged from my hiding place and cleared my throat to speak. "My thoughts on the matter—"

Thor barreled toward me. "You will have no thoughts once I crush you to pieces! This is your fault, Loki!" The thunder god raised his hand high above his head. But he paused midair as he remembered he was without his beloved hammer. His expression turned from rage to gloom.

"On that note," I said, "for once, I agreed with Heimdall. This is an excellent idea. I can use illusion magic to help with Thor's," I paused to chuckle, "wedding attire, and I will accompany him to Jotunheim as his handmaiden. I'll even wear a dress in that pretty teal he fancies me in, right, Thor?"

Thor's brow lowered. "That was a mistake. I thought you were a woman. And you swore you would never make mention of that."

"Oh, that's right, I did."

The gods and goddesses exchanged glances. Sif snorted a laugh as Thor's face turned the color of the apples that Gullinbursti munched on. Thor began to swear on everything from Sol's chariot to Odin's spear. "He looked just like a woman! I had no idea it was him! It was a mistake. I swear on Gungnir it was!"

"Right, Thor," I said to reassure him. "Never mind any of that—it's irrelevant now." Eagerly, I turned my attention to Odin for the final judgement. "Odin?"

Odin looked to Forseti, the fair-minded god who provided counsel for serious matters in Asgard.

Forseti stroked his blond beard and sent the room a nod. "I'm sorry, Thor, but this is the only way to get the hammer back."

"Agreed," said Odin. "It's an excellent idea. Prepare Thor for his wedding to Thrym. We need that hammer back."

"But, but—" Thor pleaded.

The handmaidens were already filing in with baskets of jewelry, a wedding dress, and a bridal crown with its matching veil for Thor.

We sent two ravens as messengers to Thrym that Freya had accepted his proposal and would be arriving in nine days with a handmaiden, expecting the most extravagant feast one could prepare. For the time being I remained in Asgard, afraid that if I returned home Angrboda would take my head for agreeing to this. The idea of explaining to the mother of my child that I would be acting as Thor's bridesmaid as he pretended to wed a dangerous giant didn't sound advisable. Even Angrboda had her limits.

Upon hearing the news that I would accompany Thor, I had been delighted. The opportunity to play bridesmaid for the masculine Thor was enough to make this entire calamity worth it. The day of the wedding I hurried back to my hall where I transformed myself into a beautiful maiden with long, silken hair and a shape to match my exquisite face. Carrying the teal blue train of the dress that I designed through an illusion, I met Thor outside the hall of the gods. He looked utterly ridiculous, and I stifled a cringe. The frowning Thor appeared miserable with his own attire. I, on the other hand, felt sublime.

"How do I look?" I twirled around, allowing the train of the dress to float around me in waves.

Thor muttered, "What's the matter with you?"

"That's what I thought—enchanting. All eyes will be on me. Lucky for us." Thor's thighs bulged awkwardly, protruding through the wedding gown. "Oh no, we can't have this." I snapped my fingers at the handmaidens. "Please do something with . . ." I gestured at Thor.

The Thunderer's scowl deepened as the maidens hemmed and adjusted the dress, adding extra layers to its skirts to hide his manly physique. The maidens stepped away to reveal their work. It still wasn't to my satisfaction. The thunder god's huge ears protruded from the sides of the veil.

"Let me add a finishing touch." I cast a spell to hide his ears. "That's better."

"I hate you," said Thor roughly. The god stepped awkwardly into his red and white chariot pulled by his two goats Snarler and Grinder. The train of the wedding dress got stuck under his feet as I struggled to undo it from Grinder's hungry mouth.

"For Valhalla's sake, Thor, you can't just bumble about in these garments. You have to learn to move with a bit of grace." I finally freed the dress, which was now chewed apart at the hemline, and began to carefully collect my own to step into the chariot.

A loud fart escaped Thor and he grinned at me. "How's that for grace?"

"Lovely." I made a face. "You are going to make such a treat for Thrym." The chariot jerked forward with Thor's command, and I fell into the seat next to him.

"Dressing up like this is your thing." Thor motioned at my skirts with his jeweled fingers, his knuckles stress testing Freya's emerald rings.

"It's yours now too, I suppose."

Thor's ankles stuck out from the ill-fitting ballet flats, making me sigh. This might be my most difficult trick yet.

"I just want to get this over with," he said. The thunder god slapped the reins of his two goats and the chariot lurched forward.

"Oh, come on now." I ran a comb through my hair. "It's

not so bad dressing up as a woman. I like it."

"Because you are a pervert."

We fell silent as the chariot took a turn down a dirt path that led to Bifrost. I watched as Thor reached into a wooden chest set beside him and produced a fishing lure. He looked at it briefly and then tucked it away.

"Dare I ask why you have a fishing lure with you? Planning on an excursion in between smashing a few giants?"

"I thought- "

I interrupted. "That's your first mistake. Thinking. I do the thinking you do the smashing." I adjusted my skirts from under my thighs. "You would think after all these years you would remember that by now."

Thor frowned and said nothing.

"What is it? Are you displeased with me already?" I asked.

"No."

"Thor," I said. "I can tell when you're cross."

"How so?"

"Well," I looked at Thor's huge ears. "For starters your ears are as red as Muspelheim."

Thor shifted in the seat. "I just thought perhaps we could go fishing on our return. That is, if I don't abandon you there." Under his veil, Thor's mouth turned up in a smile.

"That's not funny," I said. "You wouldn't dare leave me in a hall of angry giants."

"I would never do that."

I heard the sarcasm in his voice. "Thor, please tell me you're joking."

Thor laughed. "Only if you agree to go fishing with me."

I sighed, exhausted by his constant requests to go fishing or hunting for snakes or some other nonsense every time we traveled together. I once lost him in a forest for two hours as he chased a gigantic bullfrog that wanted nothing to do with him.

"I don't want to go fishing. These are not exactly ideal fishing conditions. Besides, you aren't dressed for it." That should silence him. Thor muttered under his breath, ending the fishing discussion.

"Speaking of being dressed for the occasion." I eyed the strand of gold around Thor's neck and recognized it as Freya's most prized piece of jewelry, the Necklace of the Brisings.

Reaching for it, I fingered it gently. "Freya lent you her beloved Brisingamen?" Its buttery-smooth surface enchanted me. I would have done anything to possess it.

Thor slapped my hand away. Sitting back, I sank into the leathery seat of the chariot, disappointed. The chariot's picked up speed, leaving behind a trail of dust as we made our way farther down the winding path.

Thor slapped the reins of the goats and with that, our speed intensified. The trail of dust became fire. I felt the chariot's wheels lift from the ground as we took to the sky towards the Bifrost which blazed in color nearby. I gripped the seat tightly as we banked left and then quickly dove down and then up again.

Lowering myself further into the chariot, I peered out to see the halls of the gods growing smaller as we climbed.

"What's wrong, Loki?" Thor asked.

My stomach in knots from the maneuvering, I gulped. "Nothing."

"For a moment there I thought you were frightened," said Thor as he directed the goats to take us into a complete vertical. Once we did, he banked us right, sending me into uncontrolled slide across the seat towards him.

"Must you do that?" I asked, pulling myself back to my side.

"Do what?"

I looked at Thor, who was chuckling to himself.

"You know exactly what I am referring to."

"Why Loki, whatever do you mean?" Thor tugged the reins, and the chariot made another sharp turn, taking us even higher. My insides churned as my eyes followed the landscape of Asgard below us: a blur of green trees, basalt rock reds, clear rushing waters, and golden fields.

"Will you go fishing with me then?" asked Thor.

"Yes, anything to get you to stop steering this chariot as if you have a death wish."

To my relief, we finally reached a large mist cloud. Above it was Bifrost and its endless arc of rainbow colors.

Once we reached the bridge Thor leveled the chariot and let out a satisfied sigh.

"Are you happy now? You got your way, and in the process, you terrorized me," I said as Bifrost burned alive under the wheels of the chariot. Below us was the formidable Kerlingarfjoll mountain range that bordered Asgard to the south. As we passed Heimdall's post, I lifted my middle finger, making sure the watchmen saw my farewell gesture before turning my attention back to Thor.

Thor's huge hand enveloped my thigh as he gave it a friendly tap. "Ah, Loki. I sure do miss traveling with you." The Thunderer looked at me with a grin.

"Can't say the feeling is mutual," I said while smoothing my dress. I inspected its windblown edges. "You know, your chariot antics have wrinkled my gown."

"Do you really think Thrym will notice your dress? This wedding will be over before it starts."

Between the howling winds I heard a rumble. The chariot shook. The Bifrost quaked.

"What was that?" I looked about but saw nothing but the colors of the rainbow bridge. "Did you hear that?"

I looked at Thor, who had one hand on his stomach.

"It was my stomach."

"That was your stomach? It sounded like an earthquake. For a moment I thought Bifrost would splinter in half."

"I'm hungry," muttered Thor.

"When are you not hungry?"

"Do you think there will be food?" asked Thor.

"Well, yes, the words wedding feast often imply food."

I sat up and slid closer to Thor.

"Speaking of wedding," I placed my hand on his silk covered thigh, "perhaps we should practice that first kiss?"

Thor's face turned beet red as he looked at me. His hands gripped the reins as he steered the goats towards Bifrost. I leaned toward him and made kissing noises.

"Kiss?" he said. "No one said anything about a kiss." Thunder boomed across Asgard's mountaintops as Thor's response to my suggestion echoed across the valleys.

"Well, what do you think you'll have to do when you marry him? Shake hands? So come on, lift up that veil of yours and—" I puckered my lips at him and batted my eyes.

Thor groaned, slapped the reins hard, and faced the skies ahead. "I truly do hate you."

We arrived in Jotunheim before sunset as expected, anxious about our plan. At least I had enough style for the two of us; Thor was supremely awkward and unfit as a bride. But we only had to carry the charade until the feast when Thrym revealed the hammer for the wedding ceremony. Once that happened, it was up to Thor to get his beloved hammer back.

He landed the chariot in a fresh pile of ox dung just outside the giant's great hall. I did my best to avoid the slop, while Thor—of course—barreled through it, ballet flats and all.

As we disembarked from the chariot, an ogre shouted our arrival. Upon his shouts several other ogres rushed past us, the ground quaking with their steps. In their arms they held baskets of straw which they scattered on the path towards the hall.

I caught up to Thor and whispered, "Don't you think it is best you lift up your skirts when walking through *shit?*" I winced as the bridal train dragged through another fresh pile of dung covered in horse flies.

"He's an ogre—they like that sort of thing. And don't speak to me, Loki. I am grim of mind."

His lack of cooperation with my suggestions wore on my patience. "Then I'm done talking to you as well."

I greeted the giants who stood at the entrance to the hall. "Greetings, please make way for the beautiful Freya, she is—" I watched in horror as Thor blundered past me, his tree trunk legs showing beneath the lace hemmed skirts he lifted, "—eager to meet her new husband." I closed my eyes hoping that when I opened them, I would see a different sight.

I did not.

The giantess with seven heads approached me. "You must be Freya's handmaiden." She pinched my cheek with warty fingers. "Aren't you a pretty little thing?"

An ogre sidled up next to me and I felt a hand on my ass. "Yes." He leered at me while licking his lips with a forked tongue. "Pretty indeed."

I stepped sideways. "Oh dear, why thank you, but I'm here on behalf of," Thor flung the door to the hall open with one hand, banging it loudly against wall, "Freya, who is very eager to meet her husband-to-be—I must go tend to her." I scurried to Thor as fast as possible and took him by the arm, but my efforts were useless. Trying to stop Thor was like a pond reed trying to stop a boulder rolling downhill—it wasn't going to happen.

We squeezed through the entrance together. The room was lit with torches that hung below enormous tapestries on the walls, each one depicting a wintry scene. A long table sat in the center of the room, set for the guests, most of whom were already eating. Servants bustled past us, dragging with them a wagon full of mead which they placed on a separate table at the front of the hall. A band in the back of the hall played music as giantesses lit candles and spread fragrant herbs about. I was relieved the scent was strong enough to conceal the smell of ox shit that Thor had dragged in.

"What are you doing, you idiot?" I hissed into Thor's enormous ear, which was still hidden by my spell. "You're going to blow this before we even take our seats." I reached up to adjust the bridal crown, falling sideways from his head as the veil stuck to his beard.

"Dear gods," I wiped the beads of sweat from my forehead with my scarf, "you are a disaster."

The edges of his mouth curled up in a smile.

"Let me do all the talking," I said in an urgent whisper, "and by Odin's beard, stop acting like a barbarian."

Servants brought in heaping trays of food and cases of ale. I could sense where Thor's attention was as his hand reached for a tray of delicacies that a servant carried by.

A voice resonated from across the hall: "Welcome!" Thrym sat at the head of the table and beside him was the giantess with seven heads. On his lap was an enormous four-eyed, striped cat. "Well come on now, over here, let me see my beautiful bride." Thrym held a fistful of food in one hand. He took a chomp on what appeared to be the leg of an ox and began to chew open-mouthed as he watched us draw closer. All eyes were on the bride as we navigated the room which was cramped with chairs, caskets of ale, and roaming giants. With a hiss, the cat left Thrym's lap when we neared.

"He is a darling, wouldn't you say?" I whispered to Thor, who muttered something from beneath the veil.

Thrym towered over us. He pulled a chair out for Thor and held out a hand to help seat his bride-to-be. I grabbed Thrym's hand and stepped between them.

"It is customary for me to sit between the betrothed and for there to be no touching until the vows are taken."

Thrym's disappointed face showed his disapproval. He leered at Thor, who sat on the other side of me with a loud creak of the chair. After another creak, I looked down to see the two rear legs of the chair splintering in half. It was too late to stop it. With a loud crackling sound, the chair fell to the ground, taking the thunder god down with it in a froth of wedding lace. Quickly I dove to tug the skirts down to conceal his legs and everything else no one needed to see.

"What kind of nonsense is this?" I yelled as we both stood, the chair in pieces. "This is the seat you chose for the most beautiful of all the goddesses, one that is flimsy and unworthy of her—" I stopped to conjure the word. Thor stood tugging the dress from between his ass cheeks —"most delicate shape?"

Thrym apologized, his voice concerned, and instructed his servants to replace the chair. Servants rushed to clean up the broken pieces and replace it with a stouter chair.

With one finger, the giant yanked the new chair closer to

him, but I yanked it back. The giant looked at me with another displeased frown.

"My apologies, mighty Thrym, but I can assure you the beautiful Freya is eager to get close to you. But she must follow the rules, right, Freya?" I gently nudged Thor in his side. His pearl-covered corset had already begun to split.

A low growl emanated from underneath the veil.

"You see," I said, "she is like an animal waiting to feel your love."

"Do tell," Thrym said, hungry for more.

I shifted away from the steaming hot breath of the giant and cleared my throat. "Of course." The stress of our situation bore down on me.

"Freya doesn't say much, does she?" asked the giantess.

"She took a vow of silence to prepare for her wedding night. It is customary."

"Well, she certainly didn't take a vow of sobriety." The giantess nodded all seven heads in Thor's direction.

Dreading what awaited me, I turned to look. Thor held a casket of mead upside down, draining its contents into his mouth, the veil pulled aside and barely covering his beard. The ale ran down his chin and into his dress in small rivulets. He set the empty casket down and let out a belch loud enough to shake the chairs. I kicked him under the table with the point of my shoe.

"You must excuse the goddess," I said to Thrym, "she's a bit thirsty. She's barely had a thing to drink since she heard the news that she will marry today."

Thrym nodded in Thor's direction. "Or eat, I suppose."

I took a deep breath, fearing what I would see next. From under his veil, Thor pulled out the skeleton of an entire salmon and just as hastily, reached for another one the size of a bed pillow. He devoured its flesh in one gulp.

I closed my eyes and cleared my throat before responding. "She's so excited she can barely keep anything down."

"I have never seen a woman eat like that before." Thrym's eyes went wide.

I couldn't tell if he was enchanted or appalled. The sweat that had formed on my brow spilled down my cheeks. I kicked Thor again and he glared at me through the veil while sucking his fingers and their glittery rings clean. "Yes, she hasn't eaten anything either. But I told her she needed to eat. She would require energy to make love to you all night, mighty Thrym."

The ogre's face went from suspicion to interest. He raised one huge, black, bristled eyebrow. "Let us begin the wedding then, shall we?"

"Yes, we should."

Thor continued eating. I took a deep breath. As usual, there was no keeping him away from the food. Dear gods, we were cutting this close. I guided a tray of pastries away from him and toward the women across the table. "Will you just stop it?" I whispered into Thor's bridal veil. "The ceremony is about to begin, and you are going to get us caught."

"Interesting," the giantess stared at both of us, "I was under the impression that Freya was one of the most beautiful of all the goddesses." Her eyes traveled to Thor's bloated ankles, which poked out from under the wedding dress. "But dare I say, she looks . . . frightening."

"She's just a bit bloated from her travels." Thor's ears protruded from the veil again. Our disguises, along with my spell, had worn thin. I began to panic. The giantess stood and circled the table. She took a hold of Thor's hand to admire the rings adorning each finger. "These rings," she said, "they barely fit on her. And that veil, it almost appears as if it is hiding a bit of facial hair."

"She is what we would consider a plentiful goddess." My eyes scanned the room, on the lookout for the hammer.

What was taking so long?

The doors to the hall opened, letting in a much-needed blast of fresh air, which I inhaled deeply. Two spotted ponies entered first, hauling a wheeled chariot guided by a giant with two corkscrew-shaped horns spiraling from the side of his head and a long black beard. One eye in the center of his forehead scanned the feast room until it landed on the bride-to-be. With a smack on the ponies' rumps, the giant directed the chariot in our direction.

Placed upon a pillow on the seat of the chariot was the hammer of the gods. Its rune-inscribed handle glinted dully in the light as the chariot neared the table. Beside me, Thor tugged at his skirts, eager to lose his disguise.

I nudged him with an elbow and whispered, "Not yet."

Thrym stood, pulling my chair out and forcing me to stand. With a huge grin on his face, he raised his drinking horn. "Ah, here is it. The hammer of the gods. Let us place it in the lap of my beautiful bride, Freya, to consecrate our vows." All the guests stood, drinking horns in hand.

The chariot stopped next to the table. Thor licked his lips at the sight of his cherished weapon.

I placed a hand on Thor's silk-covered thigh to stop him. But it was too late. He removed his bridal veil and tossed it aside into a plate of sugared pudding. I reached to pluck free the jewels that adorned its crown and quickly shoved them into the pockets of my dress. The giants gasped at the sight of the thunder god as he reached for the handle of his hammer with one huge hand.

I transformed into my own shape, but kept the dress, and ducked below the table into the shadows beside Thor as he ripped his gown apart, freeing his arm which held Mjolnir.

Thrym let out a laugh that shook the hall.

"Aye. I should have known better than to trust you, trickster of the gods. Know this, son of Odin, it was Loki who betrayed you. He has fathered a growing brood of monsters here with that ancient witch of Ironwood. "

Thor's nose twitched. His eyes lit with fury as he turned his gaze to where I hid beneath the table. I peeked out, waiting for mayhem to ensue.

"Is it too late to apologize?" I asked.

Thor let out a roar. Lightning fell from the skies, sending electricity through the hall. One bolt pierced the roof and landed on the stone statue of an oxen, splitting it in half. Thunder boomed against the walls and shook the ground. He raised his hammer high in the air and with one swing, obliterated the giantess with the seven heads.

I reached for one of my daggers, hidden in the ribbon belt that adorned my waist. I stabbed it through the sandaled foot of Thrym, who howled in pain.

The giant looked at me and smiled a toothless grin. "Hear this, Loki, son of Laufey, your monsters are prophesied to be the enemy of the gods."

I froze, dagger in hand. Prophesied to be the enemies of the gods of Asgard? I wanted an explanation, but it was too late. Thor was already raising his hammer high above the bulbous head of the giant.

That would be the last thing he said, and Mjolnir was the last thing every giant would see. One by one Thor demolished them all, each with one stroke from the mighty hammer. I watched from the safety of underneath the table, in awe at his strength.

The hall fell silent. Thor removed the rest of his wedding

garments, shredding them to pieces until there was nothing left except one sleeve and a string of pearls around his waist.

He faced the front door, naked from chest up, the remains of the tattered dress hanging from his hips. "Come out, Loki."

I crawled out from underneath the table. "Before you say anything about this, at least allow me to explain." My mind raced to conjure the words to defend my actions.

"I'm not going to kill you, Loki," said Thor, his voice cold.

I breathed a sigh of relief. "Oh, thank gods, because I really—"

Thor exited the hall without a word. Not about the stealing of the hammer, nor a question about how or why, or about Thrym's allusion to my family before Thor struck him down. I followed the thunder god as he marched to his chariot, which was parked beside a huge fountain.

The goats Snarler and Grinder were eager to be on their way, as it had begun to snow and the skies grew increasingly ominous.

"Not a word about the hammer? Not even a question as to why?" I felt desperate for him to say something. Thor climbed into his chariot and took hold of the jeweled reins.

"I am not angry with you, Loki," he said. "I thought you were my friend, and friends don't keep secrets from one another."

He looked at me with something even more terrifying than anger in his eyes—disappointment.

I had betrayed my only friend in Asgard.

"Perhaps if you allow me to explain exactly what happened—you see, I was traveling in falcon shape across Jotunheim and—"

"I don't care. You and your excuses. Your lies, your secrets, and your tricks. I have had enough. Perhaps the gods were right about you. There is no good in you after all. You don't have any friends because you don't know how to be one."

Those words hurt the most. I stood beside his chariot with the hem of the dress in my hands as a burning lump rose in my throat. This is not how I wanted things to go. "Where are you going?"

"Fishing." Thor slapped the reins, and the chariot began to move. "Alone."

He left me outside a hall filled with dead giants and demolished treasures. I collapsed onto the ground as if all my anguish converged inside of me at once. Odin's betrayal, my failures as a father, Angie's disappointment in me, and now my only friend fed up with my behavior. Even my dignity was gone.

I tried to process what I should do next, uncertain of what I really wanted. Perhaps I wasn't destined for godhood. Perhaps being a suitable father wasn't in the cards either. Perhaps Thor was right and there was no good in me. It didn't matter how much I wanted godhood or fatherhood; it was all slipping through my fingers, and now my family was in danger. And what did Thrym mean about a prophecy that my children were the enemies of the gods? I had no knowledge of this. Did Angrboda? Is that why she was so fearful of Odin knowing about our family? Was she hiding more from me yet?

I felt displaced, afraid, and regretful, as if the last hundred years had been a waste. I was torn. Should I follow Thor back to Asgard in hopes his temper would cool? Or should I return home to Angrboda and commit to my family?

After drowning myself in self-pity for some time, I took

my angst and began my long walk home, still conflicted about what to do, yet selfishly eager to feel Angrboda's embrace.

PART VI

JOURNEY INTO MADNESS

Your Ragnarok is now.
Jotunheim – Land of the Giants—That evening

L ate in the evening, I arrived at my home in Ironwood. Strands of pastel purple-tinted clouds swirled
across the sky as the setting sun cast a scarlet
glow. It had snowed since I left, quieting the forests and
blanketing everything in white. Before approaching the
front door, I stood for a moment at the edge of the birch
grove watching as smoke billowed from the roof and a soft
light radiated from the windows. Angrboda would have
questions which I had no patience to answer because I

didn't have any. I wanted to just ignore the problems as I was too ashamed to admit that I couldn't provide what she needed.

I was tired and frustrated from my exchange with Thor and afraid my family was in danger of being taken away, or worse. I was most concerned about Thrym's words to Thor, revealing my most precious secret, coupled with Baldur's increasing suspicion about my wanderings from Asgard. Would Thor tell the gods? If he did, would Angrboda's worst fears come true? What would the birth of our second child mean? Was it finally time for me to walk away from Asgard for good?

The light in our dwelling dimmed. Angrboda's shadow passed the window. I couldn't stand here forever, so I made my way through the snow to the front door. Unlatching the handle, I stepped inside, away from the cold bite of Jotunheim's air, as I had so many times before. The comforting scent of Angrboda's nightly herbs greeted me. I found Jormungandr stretched out against the threshold, asleep. Kicking my boots free from snow, I paused to look down at him; his shiny, black-scaled belly rose and fell with each breath, his eyes veiled with his milk-white lids.

"I almost stepped on you, again," I said to my unruly serpent child. "Why must you—"

"He was waiting for you, Loki," said Angrboda from our chambers, where a dim light shone. She emerged into the hearth room wearing nothing but the sheer purple nightgown that drove me mad with desire, but even that couldn't lift my spirits.

"Waiting for me? Since when does he—"

"He always does." She made her way toward me. Her belly had grown since I'd last seen her. Bending forward, she lifted the serpent into her arms to cradle him, placing a gentle kiss on his forehead. Jormungandr opened his eyes, which glowed yellow in the dark, and stared at me. "He loves you very much," said Angrboda. "He doesn't understand why you leave."

Her eyes traveled my body. "Dare I ask?"

"What?" I looked down, realizing I had forgotten to shift out of women's clothing. The teal train of my gown was bunched up at its hemline, muddied and tattered.

Angrboda raised one of her well-groomed eyebrows. Casually, I transformed out of the dress and into my usual clothing.

"It's just a bit unusual when the father of your children leaves on a quest to Asgard to steal the hammer of the gods and returns nine days later in a ball gown. Then again, I never know what to expect with you." She shook her head and with the serpent cradled in her arms, made her way to the room where his bedding was kept.

"Right, because that's what's unusual about all of this." As I followed her, I picked up one of Jormungandr's toys, a soft ring with bells on one end. My eyes landed on the remains of the pottery I had broken, which had been swept into a corner of the hearth room. "What's wrong with *this* toy?" I asked, not expecting an answer from my sleeping son as to why he chose fine housewares over his toys to play with.

Angrboda appeared at the door frame. "Oh, Loki, please, can we not get into an argument about toys and disciplining our child for one night?"

Suppressing a response that would infuriate the mother of my children, I followed her as she made her way to Jormungandr's bed, a large wicker basket with cedar shavings and a blanket. She placed him in it as I watched, feeling full of love for our child. "It's just that I don't understand him."

But I desperately wanted to. I placed the toy next to him.

"Perhaps you should take him out tomorrow, have some father and son time. He could use some stretching. It's so cramped in here. It's hindering his growth. Maybe you can take him swimming—he likes that." She tucked the blanket around the serpent as he coiled himself into rings.

"Swimming? All the lakes are frozen solid."

"Not Hestvatn."

"Hestvatn," I repeated back. "That is more like an ocean. I will lose him in there."

"You have to stay with him, Loki, not just toss him into the water and hope for the best."

Clearly her trust in my parenting was at an all-time low. I sighed. "Do you really think I would do that? Just throw our child into the ocean?"

"To be honest I don't know what you are capable of."

Frustrated, I bit my tongue. The last thing I wanted at the moment was another argument. She stroked the serpent's head and then turned her attention to me. "So, did you get what you wanted, besides a day in a lovely teal gown?" She batted her long eyelashes at me.

I looked at her and then at Jormungandr. "Not exactly what I had planned, but it will suffice."

"Do things ever go as you plan?" She lit a bowl of herbs beside our child's bed and a fragrant, calming aroma filled the room. "When you first arrived in Asgard, you were in the process of having a wall built for the gods. Next thing you knew, you were a mare birthing a foal."

I hated discussing that story more than I hated the way Odin looked at me when he needed something. "That was planned." An obvious lie. That had been a shit show that blindsided me faster than the goddess Sol travels Bifrost.

Angrboda sent me a look signaling my semantics exhausted her.

"Anyway, yes, I did fix the current problem, with one minor inconvenience or convenience, depending on how one views it."

Angrboda arched an eyebrow, inviting me to continue.

"Thor may never speak to me again. But he was irritating anyway. His voice gave me a headache, always booming and rattling my insides—not to mention his attachment to that hammer is quite unhealthy."

That wasn't the whole truth, and I knew it. Thor was irritating, but he was my friend, and his disappointment in me was a painful reminder of the many lies I had told him over the years. "Not to mention I'm tired of how he always manhandles me and whines about fishing trips. Or how he conjures rain everywhere we go. It does a number on my hair. After a while the whole thunder thing becomes a bit cliché. Good riddance."

Angrboda inclined her head and stared at me. "Are you trying to convince me or yourself?"

Damnit.

The thought that Thor might never speak to me again weighed on me almost as much as my concern for the safety of my family.

Angrboda ran her hands along my arms and moved closer until the roundness of her soft belly pushed against me. The warmth of the life inside of her comforted me more than anything had before. "I hope you stay here tonight, with us." She bit her bottom lip, a signal I knew well. My hand found the curve of her neck beneath her long, silky black hair. She could get my mind off things.

"You know what I could really use … " I hoped she would comply and drop to her knees, an enjoyable sight to behold indeed.

"What's that?" she whispered.

My eyes admired the fullness of her mouth's curves.

"That lovely mouth on my—" I stopped when her expression changed.

Her eyes narrowed as she moved away. "Why do you look like that?" she asked.

"Like what?" I peered down to ensure I hadn't accidentally shifted from a teal gown into merely a purple one—it wouldn't be the first time.

"You have this air about you, like you're hiding something. What is it?"

Witches and their damn intuition. "I'm not hiding anything."

She crossed her arms and sent me a look that dampened my arousal. "Why do you lie to me when you know that I can tell?"

I sighed. *Here it comes.* "Okay, so before you scream at me." As gently as possible, I placed my hands on her arms. The silken fabric of her nightgown felt cool against my skin, though she looked anything but that.

"I already don't like the way this sounds." Her jaw clenched. Jormungandr stirred in the basket beside us. I couldn't bear to have our son listen to yet another argument, so I led her into the hearth room.

"Look, something happened that's not really a big deal, but it's on my mind, that's all." It was a huge deal, and I couldn't stop thinking about it, but the last thing I wanted was to worry her.

"What is it?"

Could I chance another lie?

"Tell me the truth. When you take a long time to answer I already know it's because you're inventing some story."

I took a deep breath. "Thor knows about us . . . and our

children."

"Thor? Of all the gods, the mightiest, the strongest, the giant killer, son of Odin?"

I should have lied. "Just listen to me. I know Thor, and he may be the mightiest, but he is also a wheel or two short of a chariot. I'll bet by now he's forgotten all about it."

"And what if he hasn't? What if he's telling the gods of Asgard right at this very moment about us? You do realize he is strong enough to kill Jormungandr with his bare hands, don't you?"

"He wouldn't do that." The thought sickened me, putting a knot in my stomach to match the heavy feeling in my chest. If this prophecy Thrym spoke of existed, there's no telling what the gods would do—take them away, or worse. I wanted to ask her, but I was afraid it would only create strife between us.

"You just said a moment ago he is very angry with you."

"I exaggerated a bit. Not very angry, just irritated—that's completely different."

Angrboda's eyes glowed. Her clenched hands shook at her side.

Concerned about our unborn child, I tried to calm her. "Ang," I kept my voice low, "the child in your belly . . . please."

"Fix this, Loki. Fix this now. I don't care how you do it, or what it takes, but you must fix this. By the blade of my daggers, I will not live another day here in this household with you, knowing my children are not safe. Even if it means I will be forced to leave and take Jormungandr and our unborn child with me to be raised with trolls."

Angrboda spun around. I reached for her, but she recoiled from my grasp. "Ang, I just want to ask you one thing," I said as I matched her steps across the room.

"Ask me nothing, Loki! Just fix this!" She made her way into our sleeping chambers, slamming the door behind her. So much for sex.

I peeked into our son's chambers. In the dark I could see Jormungandr opening one eye and staring at me as if he knew about the deep shit I was in with his mother.

There must be a way to put our minds at ease.

It was late. Our home was silent except the gentle crackle of the fire in the center hearth. Restless, I stood over my son in the darkness, watching him sleep. My mind raced. Angrboda was right. If Thor told the gods, my family would be in danger. They might even send Thor to take him away. But *was* Thor strong enough to defeat my firstborn? I recalled the time my son dragged me across an entire snow field after the serpent escaped from my grasp, and that was when he was just two months old.

Restless, I stood to pace the room when something sharp jabbed my foot.

It was the makeshift toy Angrboda had crafted for him. A small fishing lure attached to a row of pinecones and a feather. "Jormie, you must learn to put your playthings away, I simply cannot—"

I glanced from the fishing lure to my son. Angrboda's request to take him to the lake echoed in my mind. Maybe there was still a chance that I could be a good father.

The dawn sky made me feel hopeful. Dressing quietly, I lifted him from his basket, still wrapped in a blanket, and placed him gently into an oversized provisions bag.

"Alright Jormungandr," I said as the sleeping serpent barely moved, "how about a little adventure with daddy today?"

I closed the flap to the bag. "Just us," I said, and headed out into the cold morning of Jotunheim.

We journeyed to Hestvatn, a large lake that glimmered from between two valleys. Undoing the bag, I unwound Jormungandr and placed him between two logs on the shore. He looked up at me with as confused an expression as a snake could express.

"Go on," I said, "you need to stretch out a bit and you're always asking your mother and me if you can try swimming." The serpent reluctantly entered the water, slipping into the dark lake, swimming over to a few logs.

I sat back and watched as he inspected the logs playfully. For once, he looked happy, and I felt guilty for not bringing him here sooner. Not long after, the ground began to shake. I looked up to see Thor's chariot rolling atop the mountain ridge, heading straight toward the lake.

Panicked, I called Jormungandr back to shore, but the serpent ignored my calls. I tried to lure him with the promise of playthings. "Jormungandr, if you come back now I'll give you more pottery to play in!" I knelt at the shoreline and lowered my voice as Thor's chariot drew closer. "Jormungandr," I repeated between my teeth.

The stubborn serpent was defiant and disappeared into the hollows of one of the logs instead. Thor stopped his chariot on the side of the lake across from where I stood and began to unload a rowboat.

"My, what a fine day to go fishing!" he said in a voice like thunder. Next, he unloaded a fishing rod and a lure.

Fearing for my son's safety, I couldn't just leave, so I did what I did best—used illusion to disguise myself as the dangerous giant who inhabited this mountain and with whom I shared my name. One would think Thor would find this suspicious, but I had always brought the critical thinking to our team.

"Look at this," Thor said to his goats. "What a perfect lake." He towed the boat toward shore with a pleased expression. His two goats scuttled to the water for a drink. The god looked at the boat, then looked around as if to see if anyone watched him. He picked up a fishing pole. "Looks like I might get my wish after all." He lifted the boat with one hand.

"Wait a moment," I said as I approached him. "This is not your lake."

Thor dropped the boat on the shoreline and stared at me. "It is now."

Walking closer, I towered over him in the disguise of a giant. "You must be one of the dwarves. It's a long way from Svartalheim, little fella."

Thor glared at me. "I'm not a dwarf. I am Thor, son of Odin."

"You are Thor, son of Odin?" I let out a snicker, amused that my comment got such a rise out of him. "I'm terribly sorry, I expected you to be a bit more, well, stronger. But alas, great Thor, this is my lake, and if you desire to fish in it, you must do so with me."

"And you are?" He raised a huge red eyebrow and stared at me with suspicion.

"I am Utgard-Loki, the giant of Utgard who lives beneath this mountain. You must have heard of me."

Thor scratched his beard. "Utgard-Loki?"

"Yes."

Thor blinked. He still wore some of the eyeshadow from last night's wedding. For a moment I was tempted to save him the embarrassment of returning to Asgard like that, but the feeling quickly passed.

"Well, Utgard- Loki, I'm not leaving until I go fishing."

"Very well," I replied. "Then let's be on with it, but before we begin, I should warn you, this lake is inhabited by all sorts of monstrous creatures. I would suggest rowing out to the deeper end, away from the shore, as the creatures tend to hide in the reeds."

My eyes found the shape of my firstborn as he swam along the shoreline. I blinked; it appeared as if Jormungandr had grown three times his previous length since I had set him free.

Not possible.

Thor must have sensed where my attention had shifted, for he turned to look. "What is that?" The dark shape of my serpentine child disappeared in loops and curls across the huge lake.

"An eel," I said nervously.

Thor looked unconvinced. "An eel?"

"Yes, they grow quite large in these parts. Now if you don't mind, if we're going fishing then let's get on with it. I have other things to attend to."

We dragged the boat into the water and pointed it toward the center of the lake.

"We need bait." I kept my voice casual. "How about we use your goats?" Thor loved his goats almost as much as he loved his hammer.

Thor's face flushed the color of his crimson cloak. "They are not fish bait. They are magical goats fit to pull my chariot."

"Alright then. There's some ox dung over by that wheat field—the worms in it should do the trick."

I hadn't even finished my sentence when Thor stormed off in the direction of the oxen grazing nearby. He returned moments later with the head of one of them, which he dumped onboard. The boat sank under his weight as he climbed into it and took a seat with a smile.

The smell of the bloody head tickled my nose. "I suppose that will do as well."

Before I took a seat, Thor began to row. His first stroke was so powerful it sent me to the floor.

"You don't have to row so hard." I climbed onto the other seat. "This is not a contest."

He rowed us through a patch of tall lake reeds as I searched the waters for my son. Thor stroked harder, and a fine veil of fog engulfed us. "Utgard-Loki. Any relation to Loki Laufeyson?"

I bit my lip to suppress a smile. "Not that I am aware of, although I have heard he is quite the trickster."

"You remind me of him," said Thor as he continued to row us toward the center of the lake.

"Let me guess, because of how handsome I am?" My eyes caught sight of my son, who swam past us towards another set of logs on the northernmost tip of the lake.

"More like how arrogant," Thor muttered.

The stern of the boat turned north toward the far reaches of the lake where it was bordered by mountains. "What are you doing?" I worried that he rowed too close to where I'd last seen Jormungandr.

"I want to find that eel, the one I saw by the shore."

"Then you are going the wrong way. The eels are usually that way." I pointed away from the logs where Jormungandr now swam in circles.

"But—"

"But nothing. This is my lake, my mountain. We either do this my way or not at all."

Thor frowned. "You do remind me a lot of Loki." He rowed faster.

"Do you know him well?" My eyes landed on Freya's Necklace of the Brisings, which still hugged Thor's huge neck.

"Did," said Thor. "We are no longer friends. I will never speak to him again after what he did to me. I can't trust him. No one can." He stopped rowing. The oars hung above the surface of the lake as the boat glided away from the logs. We stared at one another in the mist, the trickster in disguise and Thor, dutiful god of Asgard.

"I suppose this is a good enough spot," I said. Thor grabbed the fishing rod. He fastened the ox head to the hook and cast it into the water.

We waited.

The lake was still, the air eerily quiet. As if we were the only souls left in Jotunheim. As we sat there in silence, I felt the urge to break my illusion, to admit it was me, to explain to him all that happened, from being bribed and tricked by Thrym to explaining my most peculiar but beloved family. Thor was a father. He would understand my plight; he may even be able to give me some direction about how to be a better one. I wanted to explain it all, but the fact remained that I couldn't. He may have been my friend, but he was still the son of Odin, and his loyalty lay with the gods of Asgard, and they always would.

Thor stood and reeled the line in. He cast it again and again. Still nothing. I sat in silence watching the lake for my son, whom I could no longer see. After some moments, Thor stood and prepared to pull his line from the water for the last time.

Relieved, I said, "I suppose you are having no luck today —"

His rod began to tremble. Then it bent in half. The water rippled as the boat rocked and swayed beneath us.

"I got something." Thor reeled in his catch.

I stood, terrified, as I saw the shape of Jormungandr

writing at the end of the line.

Thor tugged, yanked, groaned, and pulled. My monstrous serpent child fought Thor as he reeled him in.

Thor slid across the boat, fighting to keep hold of the rod. "This must be a mighty big eel."

Jormungandr's head broke the surface of the water. Thor fell backward, and so did I, shocked at the size of my firstborn. He had grown four times the length of what he had been when I set him free.

My fear grew. I grabbed Thor's huge fists that clutched the end of the rod. "Perhaps you should just let it go."

He swatted me aside as if I were an insect and continued to fight with the line. The boat began to sink as my son fought back. Water flooded the hull. The ribs began to crack and splinter. Thor growled with his efforts. Sweat poured from his brow. His muscles bulged and shook. Thunder echoed up the valley. Neither one of them would give up, and it was clear there would be no winner.

"Let it go before whatever you have caught pulls us under." I fought to take control of the rod.

Thor continued to wrestle with the line as Jormungandr thrashed about. "It's some sort of sea serpent—what is it doing here?"

With lightning in his eyes, Thor stood. At that instant, the serpent lifted his head from the waters, opened his jaws with the hook through his tongue, and bit down hard on the gunwale with his giant fangs. The thunder god howled and reached for his hammer, raising it in the air.

Just as quickly, I sliced the fishing line with one of my daggers, setting Jormungandr free to swim toward the shore. Breathless, I collapsed onto the seat of the sinking boat as Thor stomped his boots and took hold of the oars.

"We are sinking, you idiot," I muttered.

He dropped the oars and stepped out of the boat into the shallow lake. With one huge hand, Thor lifted me from the boat and tossed me over his shoulder. It was humiliating, just like old times. He carried me to shore where he dropped me into a patch of tall reeds and stood facing the lake with searching eyes.

"What is it?' I asked.

"That was the biggest, strongest sea serpent I have ever seen. I want to find it again."

"Why? So, you can arm wrestle with it?" I walked over next to him.

"Snakes don't have arms." Thor spoke as if enlightening me on a little-known fact.

"You don't say."

Thick fog settled across the lake and I began to worry I wouldn't be able to find my child when it was time to return home.

"I think it would be best to let it go." I tried to discourage him. "It was merely a runt. There are many other places with even larger and mightier serpents. Those are the ones you want to test your strength against."

The god looked at me, grim-faced and brooding. "Perhaps we can go fishing again when I return?" He smiled and I sensed he knew who I really was. "You can show me where these creatures are."

I hoped he meant the invitation. "I'd like that."

Thor collected his goats and his chariot and headed south toward the ridge that led to the great sea where he would find the glowing Bifrost and his return to Asgard. I waited until his chariot disappeared over the mountains before calling to Jormungandr, who had stretched out over the logs to bask in what little sun Jotunheim had to offer.

My child looked happy. He swam toward me with a vigor

I had never seen before, as if the day of freedom in the lake to grow and roam and wrestle a god did him well. When he arrived on shore, he slithered to me. It was a chore lifting him, as he had grown so long. Despite the heaviness of the serpent, my burdens felt lighter. Some time with my son had done us both good, even if it didn't go as planned.

Before placing Jormungandr into the provisions bag, I took one last look at his sleeping face, exhausted from his efforts. He let out a low belch. While observing his size, snout to tail, I wondered if I should tell Angrboda the entire story. I doubted she would be keen on knowing I had tossed our firstborn into a huge lake unsupervised only to end up being fished out by a giant killer.

"Your mother is going to kill me, you barely fit in your basket anymore as it is." I stroked his head. "We won't tell her the entire truth. I just took you for a swim today, that's all."

The snake opened his eyes and curled his mouth in a satisfied smile. I left for home feeling a bit more certain about what I wanted.

Before the day's last light disappeared below the horizon, I stopped to reflect. Fatherhood had become my most cherished surprise. The excitement for my unborn child was building as I wondered what was in store for us all. I was eager to feel Angrboda's growing belly and to hear her approval that I had taken her advice and spent time with our son.

Reaching into the bag, I patted Jormungandr's cold snout as he looked up at me, lovingly. For once, I felt peace.

Before continuing on, I took some time to admire the shine of the sun on the Necklace of the Brisings, which now belonged to me.

It was late afternoon when I arrived back at my home. The house was in disarray and stunk of healing herbs. Beside the hearth was a chair and upon it was Angrboda's staff. Inspecting the area, I noticed a mortar of ashes. I sniffed to identify what she had been burning—herbs she used to see into the future. Placing the mortar down, I peeked into our chambers and found her asleep in our bed.

After tending to Jormungandr, I headed in to wake her.

"Ang, I'm home." My hand caressed the curve of her shoulder. She shivered. Her eyes opened. They were glassy and swollen. "Are you alright?"

"I'm fine, just feeling a bit ill, that's all." Her hand traveled under the covers to hold her belly.

"What is it? Is it our child?"

"It is. This one is more painful than our first. I just need more rest." She looked up at me. I sensed she wasn't telling me the entire truth. "Can you fetch me a tea?" she asked.

With a nod I made my way towards the hearth where several jars of healing herbs were kept. In a small vat I brewed chamomile, honey, and hyssop, a blend my mother had taught me for fevers and calming. Returning to our chambers I set the tea down on the bedside table, still wanting to ask her about the herbs I had discovered when I arrived home.

She sipped until the bowl was half drained and then rested her head, facing me.

I was hesitant to question her. "Were you . . ."

"What?"

"It's just that your staff was left out and the herbs were burned in the mortar. Were you trying to foresee our future?"

There was a long pause before she answered, as if she didn't want to tell me the truth. "I was." Her eyes traveled to the window. In them I could see tears.

"What did you see?"

She took a deep breath and looked at me with a forced smile. "Nothing. I didn't see anything. I couldn't finish the ritual. I'm too worn out." Her hand found mine; it was cold and trembling, and although I sensed her lies, I had to ask.

"Ang," I began, "I need to ask you something."

"What is it?"

"Do you know of a prophecy that foretold our children will be enemies of the gods?"

Angrboda shifted her arms against the pillow. Her forehead creased. She lowered her eyes as if searching for the answer. I could feel my heartbeat begin to thump as I awaited her response. Finally, she met my eyes.

"No, I don't. Where did you hear such a thing?"

"Thrym, right before he was demolished."

"And you believe the words of a vengeful thief at his most desperate moment?" She stroked my face with her hand.

She had a point.

"No, I don't. But I had to ask you."

"I understand," she said.

But I wasn't convinced.

"Let's talk about better things. Tell me, did you have a good day with Jormungandr?"

"I did, I took him swimming like you suggested."

Her eyes lit up like I hadn't seen in a long time and so I resisted the urge to continue questioning her about the prophecy. "You did? Did he like it?"

"Very much." I thought of his unscheduled wrestling match with Thor. "So much I think I will be taking him more often." *Minus the skirmish with a god, of course.*

"Really?" She propped up onto her elbow and smiled.

"Yes, maybe even every day."

"Does that mean what I think it does?" Her hand touched my face.

"Yes, it does." Peeling back the covers, I slipped in beside her and pulled her close to me. Her large belly filled the space between us. She laughed.

"I'm growing so large I can barely get you close enough to me," she said as we embraced. Brushing aside a piece of her silky, black hair, I kissed her.

"Close enough," I whispered.

She stared into my eyes. "If Odin couldn't kill me, then nothing can. I will be okay, and our child will be too, I promise you that."

"And I promise you that I will stay."

She narrowed her golden eyes as if she didn't believe it. "Promise?"

"Yes."

Rolling onto her side, she fell into my arms and my hands found the curve of her belly, hungry to feel the life inside of her. Proudly I told of our firstborn's growth. "Jormungandr grew. A lot. He barely fit into his basket."

"That's exciting, isn't it? He will grow to be the mightiest serpent in the entire universe. Every creature will marvel at him." She interlaced her fingers through mine and let out a satisfied sigh. "You should be proud of him."

"I am," I replied. "Very."

"Our little monster. Remember that name began as a folly because of how small he was when I birthed him. He almost fit in the palm of my hand. Now, look at him."

"He has a name to live up to."

"What shall we name our second monster?" she asked.

"I'm leaving that up to you this time."

I stared up at the ceiling thoughtfully. "I haven't given

that much thought yet."

"Do you give anything much thought?" I felt her belly quake as she laughed. "I think it likes when I laugh, I can feel it kicking about more."

"I like it too."

"Good to know, because that's the reason I fell in love in with you, because you make me laugh, much to my own chagrin." Her grey eyes sparkled to life and at that moment I was reminded how much I loved her.

Desiring more attention, I asked, "the only reason?"

"Of course not. You're cunning, lively, and of course, good looking."

"Go on."

She tapped my hand playfully. "You just enjoy the flattery."

I wouldn't deny that.

"And you understand me." She traced a fingertip across my mouth and kissed my bare shoulder, a surprisingly tender behavior for her that I secretly enjoyed.

In the moment of silence, I inhaled the scent of her hair before placing a kiss on her neck.

"What do you think our second child will be?" she asked, tugging me closer. The closeness was inviting.

"I don't care what it is."

"No? Even if it's a two-headed troll?" She laughed. "Or a beast with teeth the size of my hands?"

"Even better." I kissed her again. "All I care about is being here with you and my children, whatever they are."

"I think it's a male child," she said. "I can feel it."

"How so?"

"Because it's unruly and dramatic like its sibling." I heard affection in her voice.

My gaze traveled to one of Jormungandr's playthings on

the floor. "He's not so bad most of the time." I thought of our adventure on the lake together today.

"You must have had a really good day with Jormungandr."

"You could say that." My eyes wandered to the window where lightning streaked across the distant mountains. Regardless of what I wanted, there were too many unknowns that could alter our fate as a family. Would Thor reveal my betrayal to the gods? Was the safety of my children still at risk? Would I truly be able to control my lust for godhood? I held Angrboda a bit tighter as my fears set in.

At least for now, I had the satisfaction that only my family could provide, no matter how strange it was.

Angrboda drifted off to sleep and I was left awake with my thoughts. Quietly slipping from the bed, I tiptoed into our living room where our family stone had been placed. Kneeling down beside it, I ran my fingertips over the inscriptions. First Angrboda's name, then mine, and finally Jormungandr's. I sat back and stared at the stone, contemplating a name for our second child. After some time, I produced my dagger and one by one began to carve six runic letters into the stone.

Fehu. Ehwaz. Nauthiz. Raido. Isa. Raido.

When I finished, I sat back and stared at what I had carved before reading it aloud. "Fenrir. This will be your name, and you will be *mighty*."

"Keep a little fire burning. However small, however hidden."
—LOKI

ABOUT THE AUTHOR

A. B. Frost

A.B. Frost is a New York City native who holds a Bachelor of Fine Arts from Fordham University. She is a lover of everything Norse, long walks in the forest, chocolate, and a strong cup of coffee.

www.abfrostauthor.com
abfrostauthor@gmail.com